NATASHA JOCIC

A Stone in the Shoe

HIGHPOINT
LIT

Kay H. McCormick

This edition published by Highpoint Lit, an imprint of Highpoint Executive Publishing. For information, write to info@highpointpubs.com.

First Edition
ISBN: 978-1-7344497-8-5

Jocic, Natasha
A Stone in the Shoe

Summary: "*A Stone in the Shoe* paints a memorable picture of one woman's multifaceted life in Novi Sad, Serbia—or as the author puts it, "a Valley of Lunatics, a thousand and a half kilometers on the right bank of the Danube." —Provided by publisher.

ISBN: 978-1-7344497-8-5 (paperback)
1. Fiction 2. Literary

Library of Congress Control Number: 2021907464

Interior design by Sarah M. Clarehart

Manufactured in the United States of America

Mom and Dad, this is for you.

I want to thank my family, relatives, and friends and all the good people for their selfless support during the creation of this novel.

Natasha Jocic

Acknowledgments

I would like to thank the team at Highpoint Lit for their professional talents. I especially would like to express my gratitude to Michael Roney and Sarah Clarehart for their dedication and perfectionism. Without Highpoint, *A Stone in the Shoe* wouldn't have turned out so beautifully, and just the way I've always wanted.

1

My god, is this possible??!!!

I know this!!

This guy is writing my thoughts!

And he recognized everything I saw!

This is crazy, what is this?!!

I'm flipping through my notebooks again—maybe I misunderstood something, maybe I'm getting my period or I'm in a midlife crisis (jeez, what a horrible thought!)? But no! He has an identical way of perceiving everything, and entire sentences are outrageously the same.

After an entire fifteen minutes of pondering, I finally decided:

I'll write him a letter!

He is my James Dean who writes.

His pencils are revving and roaring.

They're breaking me.

Hi, James,

I'm Natasha. From Novi Sad. And I have no idea how to convey to you what I want to tell you so you can understand it in the right way (as I imagined it).

I've never written to a person I don't know, except for Bear Grylls, a likable English adventurer with an iron-clad stomach, and that was only on my son's behalf (I believe this information is invaluable to you, and maybe it even upsets you).

I guess you are aware of how close you are to your readers, and although we only think we know you, we are certainly complete strangers from your perspective.

But despite that, I need to write you how happy I am that there is a writer who writes because he loves it. About the life that is. I read a lot, but when I read your books I feel like I'm in the company of an old friend. I haven't felt that for a long time—that kind of belonging ...

Blah-blah...

In fact, Jamie, the truth is that I want to see you and that I don't have the patience of a saint. So, quit messing around and off you go. It will take you an hour (at most) to get to Novi Sad. Then we'll stroll down Zmaj Jovina Street, sit in a cafe in the shade, maybe somewhere next to the quay, surrounded by the divine scent of linden trees, talk a little, laugh, have a drink, hang out ...

I mean, really hang out.

Here I am, James, in my Valley of Lunatics, a thousand and a half kilometers on the right bank of the Danube. The name I mentioned originates from the locals from the surrounding hamlets, and we, who have served as their inspiration, are very proud of it. In the Valley, we are consciously and shamelessly smuggling tons of good mood, we are drenched in unreasonable laughter and soaked with pure and irreversible enjoyment.

Despite being long accustomed to my outlandish ideas, which I have in abundance (like to volunteer in Africa or establish an Animal Rescue), my relatives were in disbelief when I told them I was writing you a letter:

Natasha, you are way out of line!"

"He won't reply to you if he's the way you describe him."

"He'll think you're a teenager writing to a stranger. What do you expect?"

For a brief moment, I knew exactly how my son's friend, who cried on his own birthday, felt.

"Fuck this! Ever since I started school, everyone has been buying me only books!"

Out of a ton of enjoyment, today I used tons of paper, drained the Sun, and dragged my friends into a heated argument.

"What? She'll write THAT to him!"

"I won't let you yell at me, go, chop some wood for the barbecue, do something useful!"

My husband Momcilo, not paying much attention to the general euphoria as he sprawled on a deck chair, chimed in.

"You're still on the first page?! You will destroy the rainforests! Not enough global warming for you? You will cause an ecological catastrophe! You, a Green Guerrilla member! Shame on you..."

We were sitting on the terrace surrounded by gallons of water.
The Danube was a beast
flooded the whole of Europe
just a few of us
the dearest of the closest
Night fell
We discussed about how strong the brandy was and the distillers
    and the quality of wine
About people who are no longer with us
And yet
As if they were
We taught each other how to whistle with our fingers in our
    mouths with one finger with two fingers
Earsplitting fiercely
Where the angle of the twisted tongue
in relation to the breathing is important
We drew tempera tattoos on the skin
The fireflies were unrealistically beautiful glittering elusive dots
The stars filled the sky and came down at our fingertips
And fried fish and the brandy the Danube the poplar the acacia,
    the frogs
Mikica the Cat as the only survivor of the litter
from whom the fiercest dogs shy away
Everything smelled like us

SOMEONE felt nauseated later.
Momcilo, I'm going to die, take me to the doctor!"
"And what should I tell them? That the mother of a minor child drank too much! Shut up and vomit."
Fuck, I'm not sure how you're going to look at all this, James. What will you think? Momcilo would have risked a lot if he hadn't said on the phone: "He won't think anything. He'll read and cry."

Our small family consists of Momcilo—calm stable, good-natured—and our son, whom we once called Munchkin and Doodles and now, RAP 000 MAN or Captain Delta Force Stalingrad. Lately, he goes by the name Cile.

I work exclusively on feelings. And emotions. In Cile, I recognize something of mine, something of my husband's, but Captain is a man for himself. But not his own man yet.

Our little person.

The World Cup in soccer is about to start. Who are your favorites, if you have any, James? Or are you just enjoying on the sidelines? I don't expect too much from our team—a layer of ballet dancing, a layer of flying. Italians are my favorites because they get by and know how to do it. I could write you entire volumes about soccer, without tooting my own horn too much.

I was still in my diapers when my dad drew up the layout of players on an all-green background with sharp wooden crayons, explaining to me, with endless patience, the positions in soccer—the line of attack, defense, midfield, and everything that goes with it.

Here's my chance, Jamie. A woman who knows soccer. A shot in the goal post. A foul? That would be cheap. I don't want to knock you down. I'm just creating a little room to touch.

Do you know when you pee... Let me rephrase that since men don't pee. I don't know what you call it. When I'm dying to pee at the worst time, in a place that is absolutely not intended for doing anything, someone always stands behind me, shields me, is on guard. I'm in a hurry, I'm not squatting as I should be, my panties are halfway up my ass, streams of warm piss flood my shoes, making a treacherous trail, and the yellow drops cheerfully and unsparingly cover my helper's legs and pants.

That's how I'd guard you, James. Literally and conditionally.

Last night, Momcilo, Cile, and I were at a gig at Route 66, a bar on two levels, near the beach, known for its live music. Momcilo and his band from school days were the guests of honor. They played two or three songs, everybody was in rapture, and my husband tried his best to emulate Jerry Lee Lewis, but he forgot to set the keyboards on fire.

I was very happy when I met Jole. Out of the 24 hours in a day, Jole smiles 25 of them. He is energetic, talkative, fun. He loves to travel and does it a lot. I haven't seen him for a few months, and then he appears suddenly, just to take a break and gather strength in our town until he flies away again. He adores women and does not hesitate to court them in front of his own wife, albeit in an extremely harmless and easy way. He also adores his wife; maybe that's why he managed to have one of the few, very good marriages around. It is impossible to have a normal conversation (mistake, a usual conversation) with him.

For instance:

"Hi, Jole, I've been thinking about you these days, about that phone number..."

"I think of you every day...," he interrupts and grins.

He brings a short story, a sketch, a spark from each trip he takes.

"Sao Paulo is a fantastic city!" he shouts.

"What were you doing there, man?" I ask.

He looks at me blankly, ignores the question. OK, I didn't expect an answer.

"I stayed with some guy. Jeez, what a badass!" Jole claps his hands.

"Well-read, has a whole history in his little finger. Took me to all sorts of places. Annihilated me in pool! ME! He is a professional angler. There is no fish he didn't catch. Well-respected in the city, I tell you, everyone knows him..."

Jole paused for a moment to catch his breath and spice up the final words.

"Fuck," he said and fell silent. After five minutes, I realized that he would be silent until I threw him a question. He caught it in flight, wrapped up the answer and swirled it at my head like a Molotov cocktail.

"He's gay!" Jole blushed for some reason after this statement.

"HOW do you know, my friend?!" He doesn't answer.

"Did you see this one—her ass is singing, and those brunettes are putting their 'figs' out, to suck on them?!" he is shouting, spitting at me as he speaks. "A smart, good man, a big lad, so to speak."

He spreads his arms, he doesn't understand: "I'm sorry, Natasha, really ... too bad."

Jole and I have known each other since we were twenty years younger, twenty kilograms lighter, with 0 percent worries and 100 percent confidence that we would move the universe.

Jole was fascinated by Canada. He thought that if he just got there everything would be fine. Because everything is fine there. To keep it that way, the Canadians prepared mountains of paperwork, conditions to meet, and checks to go through. Jole started the climb. Every night, crammed around a small bar in an even smaller bar called De-Be, we eagerly waited for each report and toasted each new step towards the top. Even if there wasn't a step, we toasted anyway.

The first obstacle was money. And Jole's mom had a house. Why did she need such a big house, the upkeep is horrendous, he is her only son, the apple of her eye, who else would she help if not him... God forbid that he should beg her, that she wants him to fail, for his life to fail, for him to kill himself...

Mom sold the house.

Without having ever worked, he had to pull some strings. Pera, Djoka, Mita, or Steva. One of them had a big heart and an even bigger wallet. An empty wallet. Jole will be a chef.

How brightly the employment records shone on a dirty bar!

Get ready, frozen Ontario! Icebreaker is coming! Moms, lock up your daughters! Guys, cover your girls' necks! The Balkan vampire with drooling fangs is coming! The Balkans is fucked up. The vampire is dangerous. The vampire from the Balkans is dangerously fucked up.

And then Jole disappeared. He was nowhere to be found. For days. Weeks.

"He's a cunt, he didn't even say goodbye, I knew it..."

"You're a cunt. You would do that!"

One late afternoon, he emerged from nowhere.

"Jole, my friend, what's going on, you didn't leave, is everything OK?"

He seemed lost. Destroyed.

"I fell in love."

I'm sad today, James. I'm reading parts of your books again. And I'm sad. I do not know why. It would be more logical if I was happy, because it thrills me... it moves me a lot.

Jamie, buddy,

I find myself in the kitchen, the holy temple of every woman (the lies they tell). Momcilo went on a business trip to Belgrade or some other city, Cile is with his friend. I am sitting on a chair, staring blankly. I told Ana I would go to her place, but I don't have the strength to even fart. I'm numb. Dumb, my brother would say.

I go out on the terrace. I light a cigarette. In the building across the street, a girl is also standing on the terrace and smoking. My phone is ringing.

Ana:

"You coming?"

"No."

"What's up with you?"

"Nothing is up with me."

"Every day the same thing. Get up, eat, shit, sleep," my granny's visionary words.

My dear granny. And a town on the hill, in the winemaking region of Srem, where I spent my childhood. Rather than refer to it by name, I prefer to call it "the Village."

Hot, fragrant bread with a spread of lard, sprinkled with grounded hot paprika and big onion rings that sting the eyes—that's just one of the memories I have when I think of the Village. Even at this moment, my mouth is watering as I feel that divine taste.

Granny "struggled" with me while my mom and dad worked.

There was a real chase to find me when I decided to flee to the Wild West, by rail, across Beska. She never talked to Mile's grandmother ever again after he spat in my eye, to which I retaliated by smashing his head in. She was dressing the wounds on my arm with brandy and nettles when a horse of an old family friend Dusan bit me.

Dusan, who fought in both the First and Second World Wars, spent more than half of his life on the front line, which his wife often complained about:

"You don't know what it's like having to flee before an army, any army!"

"I heard how you women fled! You pretend to trip, fall in the grass, and continue lying there."

He had a soft spot for war songs, especially the song, "Far Away."

He had a carriage with two beautiful horses. My dear cousin Bata and I sang that song loudly, saluting him, whenever he was around, so he would allow us to get in the carriage and take the reins. He would often give me pennies.

I remember my mom's sweet laughter as she watched me run, push Bata away, and pick up pennies sticky from mulberries and dust.

Mom loved to laugh. I remember her being cheerful, with contagious laughter, unconventional, brave.

When my first-grade teacher pulled me by the hair (and I wasn't the only one she did that to because, at that time, that was an integral part of education) all the parents protested from afar. Only my mom marched straight to the principal's office. My mom pulled me out of school, she wrote absence notes herself so I could practice conversing in English with people from foreign countries during the international table tennis competition, which was held in Novi Sad, while Russian was still the predominant foreign language in schools. I had the right to soil a new dress.

"Let her play, childhood goes by fast."

She would dress me in clothes that were comfortable, and on festive occasions, encouraged me to think with my head and say what I think. Mom also encouraged me in my early literary endeavors and listened to my epic stories for days, the meaning of which I could not figure out myself.

When I started school, I used to go the Village only on weekends and during school breaks. My granny used to tell me:

"My precious, I love it when you come but I also shiver inside!"

2

When my mom, my granny's eldest daughter, died, Granny followed me around like a shadow.

After having a public kiss with the most desirable Village slicker, I received valuable instructions:

"If you marry someone, it doesn't have to be a ball and chain."

She personally threw a bucket full of chicken offal on the head of the most popular swindler in Srem because he pinched my ass at a Village party.

My granny had a trusted partner in all of this—her younger daughter, my aunt. My granny had my back. My aunt had my hips.

Going out on the town? Sure, why not—but with Bata. Going on a summer vacation? Of course—with Bata. Who could take better care of me than her son? He would shoo me into some dark corner of a bar, shove a glass of juice in my hand and say, "You don't hear what you hear, you don't see what you see!"

The only thing I saw was his friends. They were all so cute and distant. Even if some of them were to peek into my dark corner, it was only to check if the waiter warmed up my juice enough, I was annoyed.

My mom, aunt, and granny gifted me security. My dad gifted me trust.

Dad and I grew apart somewhat after mom died. I grew apart.

"Natasha, Mom is very ill and will not recover," he told me then.

I hated him. It is as if he personally passed the verdict. I wanted to hear from someone who would annul the ruling and ask for a retrial. To pretend that nothing happened.

Milan always accepted things as they were. Brutal. Painfully realistic.

If they agreed with him, the better. If not, he would put his cowboy hat on, put his feet on the table and laugh:

"It's all rock and roll, my beautiful boy."

That's what he called me: "My beautiful boy."

When it rains
I put a hat on my head
My father had a cowboy hat
Helped me make my own
I'm still learning how to wear it
But it's there
Everyone has a hat
It's a matter of decision

We are travelling to the coastline, Mom, Dad, and me. We are singing. Mom and I need to pee but Milan doesn't care as he's rumbling along roads:

"You can pee in your pants, you Betsy Wetsies!"

I am sitting in Mika Antić's lap and reciting a poem with him. Mom and Dad are laughing. Antić was a Serbian poet, film director, journalist and painter, and a major figure of the Yugoslav Black Wave. He was especially known for his poems about Romani people and for teenagers. Mika Antić was a real bohemian.

A gypsy orchestra is playing for us in a tavern. Milan wants them to sing the song called "Green Eyes" and my mother's emerald-colored eyes start radiating like a thousand diamonds. He is sticking bank notes on the musicians' sweaty foreheads.

I am thrilled:

"I wanna be a gypsy!"

I was younger than Cile when a boy from the neighborhood was pestering me:

"Daaad! Go tell him!"

He didn't even lift his eyes off the newspaper.

"Don't wail like a banshee, you're a big girl, go out and tell him yourself!"

I collided with my mom at the door, she was already on her way to tell the boy off, I ran out into the yard, dealt with it myself, and then bumped into my dad at the door. He was on his way out to buy cigarettes and a newspaper.

We are waiting for the broadcast of the Muhammad Ali-Joe Fraser boxing match:

"Who are we rooting for?" I ask.

"Fraser chews gum, plays the guitar, and jokes around," my mom has already picked the winner.

"And who will win?"

"The better one will win." Milan is relentless.

Today I am traveling to Sonja's in Pancevo. Sonja lives with her parents and son Petar, Cile's peer. She's divorced. Has a boyfriend whom she sees when she wants to.

I envy her a little bit on that.

I met Sonja two years ago, but we have known each other our whole lives.

Sonja's life was marked by the music and friendship with the singer Meri Cetinić.

As a twelve-year-old, she first heard Meri in concert in the city of Split, Croatia. She bought all the albums, cut out newspaper articles and was always in the front rows at concerts. After Sonja wrote the 150th letter to Meri, she finally replied to her.

For God's sake, James, don't use this for wrong purposes.

A month ago, Sonja visited Meri on the island of Korcula and spent an unforgettable day there. On my dresser I have a postcard of this beautiful island where the sea smells wonderful and invites you to take it easy.

Cile picks what he will bring with him. Ten marbles, five of each kind. A gun. Definitely a cell phone, which is his staple.

I call Sonja to let her know when we're leaving. Petar picks up the phone.

"Hi, Petar, guess who it is—you have three chances. If you are right, you get a little prize," I say.

"I know!" Petar sounds cheerful" It's Natasha from Novi Sad!"

"Well done, Petar, right on the first guess!"

"Well, it's not me. Our phone has a caller ID," Petar blurts out. "Do I still get the prize?"

I really like Sonja and I am looking forward to seeing her. I look forward to the trip as well. Sometimes I almost feel sad when I get to my destination, no matter which one. I want to just continue driving, without stopping anywhere, as the road takes me.

> I have a stone in my shoe
> I am often in a hurry
> And I hate to stop
> I bend down as I walk
> But the stone crawls up between my fingers
> Or gets into the fancy holes of my sneakers
> Sometimes it tickles me
> Sometimes it pinches me
> It's almost fused with my skin
> It always on the road with me

Sonja and I talked about all the important issues. We came to conclusions. Exchanged books. Encouraged each other for the days to come. My friend. One of the few people who regularly reads. An accomplice. If I were, by chance, a bank robber, I would choose her as my companion.

I'm a little nervous at the thought of you reading this letter, Jamie. I am a nervous wreck. And I'm scared.

"If anyone should be afraid, it's him!," Bata teases me. "I'm going to warn him not to take the letter, he should flee the city... So what, we are going to apologize to the man? It's not our fault. Alas, he will even sue us for the stress he suffered, I will have to sell the land and the house, leave my children without inheritance, I love you too, but I don't attack you!"

I feel like paying someone to write on my behalf.

Once upon a time there were professional scribes. They helped illiterate people. They read and wrote letters for them. They charged for their services. Something like today's lawyers.

The people were grateful to them to the heavens.

The heavens were grateful to the people.

"We are all slaves, my boy," Milan said as I cried over *Uncle Tom's Cabin*. "Only the color of our skin distinguishes us. If we were not slaves to ourselves, we would have no problem with masters."

"Live the gun, take the cannoli!"

My god, what a movie! What badass actors, James! When I first saw

The Godfather I was determined to marry a mobster, from Sicily, no more or less.

"Fortunately, you did not. If you did, terror would have reigned, half the city would have been mutilated!" (Thanks, Bata.)

You don't even have to bring cakes, James, I have cakes, my house is made of cakes, I'm a cake. I am even going to get a gun—just in case... *Capisci?*

I hope this letter will not "sleep with the fishes," Jamie, decomposing slowly on the muddy bottom.

I also read it to Momcilo, he gave me a couple of guidelines:

"You are really roping him in, aren't you?"

All of this is really entertaining to him. He knows me well enough. And he knows.

The Earth is spinning
Seven billion people are spinning with it
Animals
Insects
Forests
Canyons
Oceans
You and me both
We are making love
What a miracle that is

Cile came home from school laughing:

"Mom, do you know what happened today? The teacher asked what is the synonym for the word 'writer' and Nikola burst out 'A doodler!'"

My shit froze in my pants.

Maybe I'm a doodler too.

That wouldn't be good, Jamie. Not for me, let alone for you! That would not be good at all.

I heard on the radio that some bigshot bought a part of the Moon for his last fiancée. The fiancée was touched, the public went crazy, the customer was proud. The Moon is silent.

Nobody asked it anything. And there is nothing to say anyway.

I am not drawing a parallel, but this reminded me of an anecdote that my dad told me a long time ago, prompted by my pestering him to buy me I can't remember what.

Overall misery prevailed immediately after the end of the Second World War. People were happy with one loaf of stale bread, which was supposed to last a week. One day, new neighbors moved to Milan's area, making a lot of noise. They unloaded a lot of things from the truck and brought them into their house: a stove, a gramophone, big mirrors... My father, like other children, started salivating when he saw a leather soccer ball. A real ball. The realest possible. Untouched, fragrant. Just like they imagined in their boyhood dreams.

The children started badgering their parents for the ball, the parents pestered their children. "Maybe that sounds ridiculous today, Natasha," Milan mused, "but everybody first started whispering about that ball, then talking loudly, and then it got to the point where the adults met and discussed what to do next."

At the end of this sob story, leading a crowd of children, Dad's grandfather knocked on the door of the new neighbors. He asked to see the ball. After they handed it over to him distrustfully, he took it in his hands, turned it around, stared at it, assessed it.

And made a decision:

"And THAT'S the ball! Don't make us buy two of these for each one of you."

Everyone was relieved, peace was restored, the children continued to shoot their rag balls.

My eyes are fixed on the big clock in the living room. I set myself a goal: one cigarette every two hours. I'm checking the batteries. Shitty clock! I'm checking the time on my cell phone. What is this, a conspiracy? Cile tells me a joke. Don't start clucking now, kid. There's this letter too...I'd rather burn it!

Marina sends me a message:

"Two tickets for the theater, a great show tonight, okay?" Marina's good friend works at the Serbian National Theater, often procuring free tickets.

She must be crazy. I am not going anywhere. I don't hear anything. Don't fuck with me. I type a reply:

"I'm busy, another time."

"Why, what are you doing?"

"Waiting."

Whenever we were supposed to go the Village, Momcilo usually had urgent obligations. Incredible! After so many years, he still comes back from there dazed and with progressive hearing loss, he claims.

When he went there for the first time, on an official visit to meet my family from my mom's side... Fuck it!

He barged in just at the moment when the debate about Djokara reached its peak.

Only a day earlier, Djokara shot the worker of the local power company in the leg for trying to cut wires on his power pole because of months' worth of unpaid electric bills. The conversation went on roughly like this:

"He shouldn't have shot him in the leg first; could've fired in the air, to warn him...."

"Well, he did warn him. Of course he did—he saw the gun, didn't he?!"

"I feel sorry for the boy, it's not his fault, he did as ordered..." Women were a bit softer.

"Fuck him and those orders!"

"He could've lost his job..."

"He would've found a new one, look at us, none of us is lazy, we're all working..."

They turned to Momcilo:

"Sit down, you rascal, relax..." They're eyeing him up and down.

"So, you're the one! Natasha's guy! What d'ya want?"

Momcilo is struggling to understand them. Grammar is not his strong suit and he cannot remember that cases are used in that way.

"What are you drinking, boy? Speak up!"

They took him to a liquor store later.

So as not to turn out to be very backward, he knocked on a barrel to...he didn't even know what he really wanted.

"Stop!" They jumped at him.

"You don't knock on the barrel!"

Momcilo could see himself cut into pieces, stuffed in one of those barrels.

"You caress the barrel, you kiss the barrel." They instruct him and demonstrate how it should be done.

"You drink from the barrel…"

As punishment, Momcilo had to drink. From a monstrously long pipette, which ended directly in his stomach.

He was not left in the lurch, they followed him closely: "Have another one. To hell with it!"

Bata, then already married, hugged him tightly:

"You've been screwed over, my friend, mark my words, you've been fucked over, don't pretend later nobody told you… My sister is, if at all possible, an even worse villain than this sturmführer," he nodded to his wife Sandra.

Bata and I often exchanged glances while standing on the stairs in front of the house in the Village. I know he thinks the same as I do. How the fuck did we end up in chicken coops when our White Dove ranch was so perfect?

Everyone loves Djokara. Few invite him to their homes. One day, Djokara told his boss that he was a piece of shit, that he didn't want to stink of his crap anymore, and he went home to wash himself.

"The whole *world* of knowledge is *not worth* the *tears* of a little *child*," he quoted Dostoevsky, sold a good piece of land and donated all the money to children whose parents were killed in the wars.

He nicely explained to his best friend that he was a cunt because he was gossiping behind his back, and then he kicked him in the butt, out of the yard. An incurable gambler. He was investing the truth, he should have gotten justice.

> They say he's a loser. I wouldn't know that. I know Djokara tried.
> He rolled his dice.
> Do not seek consolation
> Don't cry over evergreens
> Dance in rhythm
> Dance through time
> Relaxed
> Play

We are going to Ana's daughter Olja's birthday party. Cile insists on personally wrapping the present. He crumpled the wrapping paper, using up all the duct tape.

"Why do girls like to put on make-up and dress nicely?" he asks me.

"Everyone likes to look beautiful." I suspect that this is not the end of his questions.

"Even when it hurts?"

"What do you mean?"

"Olja told me that she always wants to cry when her mother combs and does her hair, she just suffers because she knows she'll be beautiful."

"You must suffer for beauty."

"Good thing I'm not a girl!" Cile thanked the chromosome game.

I told Ana that.

"You know he's right. Remember how we were," she says.

"There is nothing to remember, I'm hallucinating from hunger, I've been on a diet for seventeen days now!"

Ana looks at me, I can feel that she is going to blurt something out.

"Only your eyes remain."

I used to be able to go hungry for days. Because of reciprocated love, because of unrequited love. Mostly because of unrequited love.

Ana: "Did he call?"

"I do not know! My phone is always busy."

I charged at the little red phone like a wild bull.

"Dad, I can't stand that idiot anymore. Whenever I am waiting for the phone call, she calls."

"The only problem is that you're always waiting for the phone, Natasha."

Spectacular nights on the town.

The main characters: Ana, Marina, Tijana, and me. Gathering place: my house. Where we had the best time, in most cases.

"Four musketeers!" I shouted.

"Four Graces." Ana has always been a more romantic one.

Long arduous hours of putting on make-up, conspiracy plans, perfumes, curlers, let alone choosing what to wear—a never ending story.

While applying mascara for the thirtieth time, her eyes popping out as she looks herself in the mirror, Tijana sighs and consoles herself. "Thank God we are beautiful! Imagine how much time unfortunate looking girls need to get ready."

We are finally ready sometime before midnight. Barely. As we went out, Milan would mimic the sound of a military trumpet:

"Too-too-too-too-tooooom! Attack! To victory!"

Usually we only exchanged glances with cute "alley cats" from Novi Sad and didn't need other company.

From time to time, a "wolf" would drop in. The first thing he did was to separate one of us from the herd. At night he would lure her and drag her to a lonely, erotic place.

When a sheep is aware that it is a sheep, it makes things a little easier. We wore old, torn panties, preferably with gray worn rubber at such rendezvous. The chastity belt itself could not be as efficient.

Momcilo is, without realizing, partly responsible for my diet. Sprawled in an armchair, wearing shorts and a bra, I am nibbling on chips. All the lights were on. The apartment was bright. Momcilo's gaze would envelop me from head to toe.

"We all seem to have put on a little weight over the winter..." he says.

I promised myself that he would look at me differently next time. In that way. Until then, he would look at me only in the darkness and shadows of the bedroom.

Maybe I'm still in love with my husband? That would be really nice.

"How ludicrous and silly we were... And how many tears we shed because of ... the bastards!" Ana's husband, Ivan, screwed something up.

"We had Milan," I say.

Her gaze softened, her lips parted in a smile: "Yes, we had Milan."

"Come on, girls. Put on 'Crying Time,' cry your eyes out with Ray Charles, read a poem, write a few verses, and then run to the bathroom to rinse your faces and put on makeup. In that order!"

God, James, you'll think I'm a fat, stupid whiner that all the guys rejected even when I was at my best!

We are spread over the Boulevard
We are crawling moseying
The young, the old
Puppies sparrows
There are fewer and fewer of them by the way
And no one pays attention to that
Everyone has a story to tell
That they think is special
Thinking and shitting is not the same

3

My first poetry reading was pretty hazy to me. The only thing I remember crystal clear is the angry face of my "mentor." How upset, almost offended, he was as he was trying to explain to me why I had to come in a mini skirt, not jeans.

He had yellow teeth and bad breath. Today he is all smiles on the cover of his book in bookstore windows. His teeth are bright white.

I don't know what his breath is like.

"Readers don't want your butterflies, they couldn't give a shit about your dreams!" he shouted. "Give them sex and blood, they don't care about anything else!"

Am I entering into a fight arena, a strip club, or a seedy bar next to the highway?

"Let them look you in the eye," he insulted me with his breath, frantically pulling my shirt down.

It was probably a third time (I cannot remember exactly) when I took the microphone in my hands and knew what I had to do.

I removed the bangs from my forehead, on which I had drawn two pink breasts:

"This is for you to look me in the eye!

"And this is for you to hear me: DICK PUSSY SHIT TITS!

"You will have to take care of the blood yourself!"

I went back to my butterflies. I kissed the picture hanging on the wall of modernist Swiss-born novelist and poet Blaise Cendrar.

I could have sworn he winked at me.

I went home and told my dad what happened.

"That's nothing that people haven't seen before, my boy. Nothing they haven't seen before," Milan commented.

"And people are disgusting!" I was on the verge of crying.

"Sometimes they are heroes, sometimes traitors. The world is not black and white."

Mine was blurry and smudged. The colors blended chaotically into each other. Tornadoes and rainbows.

When I look at Bata's son, Nemanja, my nephew, (who's twenty-three years old) as he mixes his own colors, I have an irresistible desire to tell him:

"Take it easy. Why are you rushing so much? Enjoy!"

Even if I told him, he wouldn't hear me. It's better that way.

I was eighteen when Nemanja was born. As a child, he called me "Nana Your." ("Go to Nana Your and whine to her.").

I took him to "parties"—that's what he called going to the circus, the zoo, fishing, trips. When Sandra smacked him (he spilled the contents of his potty, which was full to the brim, in the middle of the carpet), I demonstratively took him away and had a serious quarrel with her for the first time.

Once, while Tijana and I were in her tiny kitchen, with cups of coffee turned upside down, talking about who, with whom, where and how, Nemanja fell asleep in my lap.

"My sugar bugs, why aren't you talking?" We gathered around him.

"And whom should I talk to?" he asked us sadly.

And whom should I talk to, James? This question still haunts me to this day.

"Are you listening to me? I am talking to you!" (my aunt's usual yackety-yack).

When Nemanja was in high school, I got him absence notes.

"Nana, I need it just for today, I have to go to that soccer game..."

"No problem. Scram!"

"Nana, thank you! Can I get one for tomorrow too?"

His coming of age, a driver's license, a big party, and going through a yellow light in front of an ambush—the police...

"Nana, do you know anyone in the police? I didn't see the yellow light, I swear... Don't tell my mom."

He didn't see the entire traffic light.

"I don't," I replied.

Dead silence on the other end of the phone.

"But I know who has. And he owes me a favor" (*The Godfather*, you're the king!).

Nemanja is that one-in-a-million who has empathy or "the process of directly immersing oneself in emotional states, opinions and behaviors of other people," as the scientific definition goes.

He gives up his seat on the bus to seniors. He is the only person who visits sick friends. He covers for his younger sister Isidora when she messes something up.

Nemanja gives and does these things without the least hesitation. He babysits Cile when Momcilo and I are busy at the same time. He lays out juices, fruity, carbonated, a variety of salty snacks, chocolates.

When Milan died he was the first person at my door.

Nemanja was the only one who was able to say things like, "Many of my friends' grandparents pee in diapers, are spoonfed, and avoid being hit with a stick. They haven't really lived for a long time, but they won't die. Your dad spent his time in company of young people, drank a couple of brandies, listened to tambourines, went home and died."

I can proudly say that our relationship is on a higher level than that of the usual aunt and nephew. We are friends.

I would give one of my hands for Cile. The other for Nemanja.

It's raining. Pouring. As if water curtains are coming down. The news reports that the cyclone is coming from the Pacific. It traveled a long way to get to Novi Sad. I go out on the terrace and unbutton my shirt. Big raindrops are falling on my neck, chest, stomach.

I am dragging this letter out as if there's no tomorrow, Jamie, and I didn't even tell you the most important thing.

James, I'm beautiful. I don't just have beautiful eyes. People turn back to look at me. Back in the day I knew why they did that. Today, I no longer know—maybe I have a stain or am wearing my shirt upside down.

Cile takes after Milan:

"My mother is beautiful. But she looks better dressed than in a bathing suit."

"Pick the scent of the soap I am going to wash your mouth with, son. Strawberry, honey, or the homemade one with lard—made in the Village."

We are all dressed. And trained. We bury ourselves in piles of clothes. We sew. We glue on. Layers long enough to wrap the Great Wall of China at least ten times. Packed in, tucked in. Branded. Just for show. No one talks. Let alone listens. If we were to remove all these layers, we would be little, very little.

Let's rip off all those rags, James, tear them off, strip naked and go underground! After the first shock, we might learn the art of listening again.

"I would like to talk a little," I whispered in the ear of a bad boy from Novi Sad on our first date.

"Go ahead, talk, I don't mind," he muttered and continued to tuck his hand under my skirt.

I didn't fuck him then or ever, because I thought I was in love and holding out was the right thing to do. For him, who banged everything that moved, it was a revelation. Long after that, he told me in detail who he fucked, spicing the stories up with tasteless details.

"I only trust you," he leaned toward my ear and intoxicated me with his scent.

He didn't even brush against my panties and yet he fucked me over. Totally!

They wanted sex. We were, so to speak, also an interested party. With the one who will call tomorrow.

Milan also warned me:

Young Mela's hand was asked in marriage by boys from another town. Mela wanted to do it. She would marry, get a gold ring, wouldn't have to do anything at all ever, and live like a lady. Mela's brothers were fiercely against it:

"Don't go, Mela. They are lying to you, Mela. They don't want to marry you, Mela, they want to bonk you!"

Who could have known that better than him?

One of the few business owners in Tito's time (Tito was the president of former Yuogoslav), he spent his working life in his workshop. He awkwardly hid his short-lived romances from me because he thought I was too young to know about them.

4

It's Sunday. Milan is brushing his teeth loudly. Gurgling and whistling are coming out of the bathroom in a cloud of perfume. He puts on a navy-blue suit and a tie the color of dark cherries. Shoes of identical shade are sparkling on his feet. "Where are you going?" I ask.

"To the workshop." He doesn't even blink.

"At Sunday noon?"

He looks at me reproachfully: "Someone has to work in this country." On the phone, he uses the codeword "bro" when talking to his "workshops."

"Where are you at, bro? We're still on for tomorrow?"

Later, this flattering title was replaced by real names. Aunt Ruža, Aunt Bosiljka, Aunt Gospava. I only knew their voices, imagined their looks and features.

"They're all bros, my little boy. Nothing more than that." Whatever that meant. And it meant the following:

"Natasha, if Aunt Bojana calls, tell her that dad is not at home."

"I told her that two hours ago and an hour ago, and fifteen minutes ago!"

He shot them down like clay pigeons.

"What's the catch?" I really wanted to know.

"No catch," Milan replied. "Uncrowned self-proclaimed princesses are looking for a kingdom. That's all."

That's all? How many of us there are, us, the princesses, and yet we don't even realize that we are actually "bros"!

When I met Momcilo, I was neither. I was Natasha.

Momcilo wanted me to be just Natasha (and now, occasionally, he wants me to be that). He was the only guy to have read the book *Six Problems for Don Isidro Parodi*, written by two geniuses, Borges and Casares. I read "his" book—*A Brief History of Time* by Stephen Hawking (it seemed too long to me).

Momcilo and I are constantly reading each other. We cross each other out, we write words to each other, scribble, supplement. Some parts are comedies, some real love stories, and some creepy thrillers, with a serious hint of horror.

Cile has discovered Facebook. He's been chatting with Denis for two days now, planning to meet.

"Did you finally arrange it?" I ask him.

"Nope."

"What's with all the messaging then?"

"We're still arranging."

Anja, his school friend, sent him an e-mail:

"Are you coming to Lijana's birthday to cause some chaos?"

"Who's Lijana?" Cile asks.

"Tijana. Yes or no?"

"Who with?" he asks cautiously (I guess).

"With Nena and mine."

The phone is ringing. It's Tanja, mother of Cile's school friend Saska. On Thursday, Saska suddenly decided not to go on a school trip on Friday. Tanja invented an excuse for the teacher—Saska is abroad. Saska's friends called her from the school trip but she forgot where she was.

Tanja is annoyed.

"Stupid girl! I will turn out to be a liar because of her. That child will be the end of me... What are you doing?"

"I'm freezing. Isn't the weather horrible?"

"Oh, I already have a headache from everything, I had one yesterday too. Fuck the rain and winter, I had to turn on the heating... It's always my fault... Argh! Come over for a coffee..."

"Will do."

"Cile, do you want to come to Saska's with me?" I ask him.

"Hell no!"

"Well, you've been whining you're bored."

"I'd rather be bored by myself than with Saska."

Be objective but gentle, Jamie.

Am I boring?

We used to visit my mom's Aunt Stana and her husband Zdravko in Belgrade every month or so. They did not have children. Nor were they apt to be parents. Which is irrelevant. I was indescribably bored there, and I always presented impossible conditions in exchange for my willingness to go.

"I'll go if ... you buy me a baby tiger for my birthday."

After a hearty lunch, cakes and coffee, rounded off with a conversation, we are getting ready to head home. Stana and Zdravko protest:

"Stay a little longer. Why are you so boring?!"

"How come we are boring and they are bothering us?" I was one being annoying on our way home.

Who is boring to whom?

I failed to grasp it then. I fail to grasp it now.

5

Sonja's mother Gordana is in the hospital in Novi Sad. No big deal, she has benign polyps in her nose. She will spend the night at the ENT ward. The doctors will laser out her polyps and she will be released home ("to play"). Of course, I'll visit her.

As I am approaching the hospital I feel nauseous. Milan had surgery there not so long ago. I stop at a store on hospital grounds and buy a newspaper and a juice box. Anger overwhelms me. What shitheads! All the stuff here is twice as expensive as in any other shop in the town. Isn't it enough that people here are sick?! They are already paying dearly for their lives.

I rummage through the hallways looking for Gordana.

"What are you doing here?" the nurse hissed. She stood right in front of me with her hands on her hips like a sumo wrestler. After my short explanation, she answers with an even shorter sentence and says that Gordana was released from the hospital. No, she was not operated on; the laser device broke down and no, nobody knows when it will be repaired.

I rush to the exit, I see patients with their strikingly yellow faces, sitting, lying in their rooms. Lonely. Isolated. Loud music is heard from the nursing room, a total disaster for hearing and nerves.

My stomach cramps and twists, I run outside and vomit on my sneakers, on the sidewalk, on this day.

I open the front door of my building. The door is opened from the inside by pressing a button, and a key is needed to open it from the outside.

An old lady, with a big bag on wheels and a stick, is waiting in front of the door for me to open it for her. We pass each other. "Thank you," she smiles. "We're always looking for that key."

I was really moved by her words. We are all different, and yet we are looking for the same thing.

Everyone needs a key, but it's a different key for everyone.

The farmers market is crowded. A colorful variety of fruits, vegetables, and flowers. A crumpled, shrunken woman sells flowers in front of the market. I can't tell her age. There are not many flowers in front of her, only two buckets full, but they are fresh, of beautiful colors, and large. The gray cat walks around her legs, then dips its head into one of the buckets and drinks water. Flowers cover half of her body like a wreath. A woman blinks staring at the sun. I take a mental picture of that.

There are days that resemble Sundays. Monday, Wednesday, Friday, regardless. When I leave the apartment, I step into a Sunday. People walk as if it were Sunday, the leaves rustle like it's Sunday. Why is that so and why exactly Sunday? I have no explanation at all.

I have something to tell you, James. It's uncomfortable. I lied to you, didn't just write to Bear Grylls. I also wrote to Steve Irwin. And wanted to write the Dalai Lama.

Stevie, a great Australian protector of crocodiles and animals in general, and a great man overall, was an idol of our whole family.

We never missed his adventures on Animal Planet.

Every now and then, rumors could be heard of his alleged death. I quickly wrote a short e-mail and sent it to Stevie's address, on the other side of the world, in Australia. We were literally jumping for joy when he soon replied with kind, warm words:

"Ha-ha... Stevie was bitten by a venomous snake and the lizard was the end of him?!"

He was extremely honored by our e-mail, and he asked us to write our postal address, so he could send us small souvenirs.

The correspondence from us went like this:

"Cile caught two lizards and a grass snake (which he held in his hand for a whole second)."

"Orphaned elephants have arrived at the zoo."

A year later, Stevie died.

"Mom, maybe it's a scam again, you know, those nasty rumors..." Cile was hopeful.

It is a scam. Of the ultimate kind. Stevie left doing what he loves. And he loved everything that is good, beautiful, and noble. The great Stevie! He tricked death.

Personally, I don't know a single person, including myself, who knows what it is that they really like to do.

Even today, our families keep in contact. Merry Christmas, Happy New Year, but it's just not the same thing anymore.

I wanted to write an e-mail to the Dalai Lama, whom I have always admired, to show my support for the protests of Buddhist priests in Lhasa.

I was stopped by the response he gave to a public question asked by the popular American actor, Richard Gere (a self-proclaimed Buddhist):"How can I help you?"

"Everyone should do their job," the Dalai Lama remarked to him.

Well, I am doing my job, I am hard at it, I don't let myself be distracted. I'm writing you a letter, Jamesy.

I take the bus. Reluctantly. I avoid buses, too many people in a cramped space. I look at the dirty window. It is so muddy that it is impossible to see through it.

Who maintains them? I don't want to even think about what the bus engine looks like from the inside.

A scream interrupts the murmur of the crowd.

"Aaaaahhh!" Slap! Scream. Slap! Bam!

"Shut up, you shut up right away!"

I turn around with trepidation and see the largest, bulkiest, the most enormous woman. How did she get on the bus?

She mercilessly pounded the child on her lap.

"I'm thirsty too but I am not whining." Slap! Bam!

Other passengers are not reacting. A group of young men are talking about soccer, some are tapping on their mobile phones, most are reluctantly staring into the distance.

They just aren't there.

I approach the mountain of the woman:

"Ma'am (?!), maybe you should try to tell him a story, sing him a song?"

She gets up. Jesus, even her shadow is heavy, bigger than the whole bus! We are going to roll over!

"Mind your own business!" she's spitting her venom towards me.

"If you touch that child one more time, I will call child protective services and I will watch with great pleasure as they take him away from you!"

She couldn't have known if I was serious, or she'd slap me around too. She returned to her seat and fell silent. The hitting stopped.

"It's not worth it, ma'am. They hit their kids too. Everybody does. Hey, if you were mine ... I would chop your hands off! You pig! Do you have some change to spare?" a gypsy boy chimes in, peeking out from the back seats.

Why did the three little pigs run away from home?

Because their parents are pigs.

Our friends are getting ready to leave for their summer vacation.

I call them to wish them happy travels and nice weather.

Dragan answers.

"What's up, travelers?" I ask.

"Here, Natalija is making lists, shopping, packing. I am burning CDs. We shipped the kids to the grandmother's."

"Natalija is messing around and you're struggling."

"I'm shedding blood, at her orders! She is the one who chooses the music," says Dragan.

"Are you coming back for the Exit festival?"

"Yeah, right."

"Dragan, we had the same conversation last summer! Discs, packing, remember?"

"Fuck it, we did!" Dragan remembers all of a sudden.

"And we'll have it next summer too."

"Ah, no. There will be no discs next summer. Next summer, this old man will pay for a cruise on the Nile! Watch this space!" Dragan is not joking.

We have added another topic for next year. The same one.

6

I remember Momcilo, Cile and I, together with our good friends, Jasna and Jovan, are on the coastline, deep inside Greece, right behind Athens.

The place was not on the map. It was an original fishing village. Locals, pines and us. No crowds, no pedal boats, no car rentals, no mopeds, no bikes, no donuts, no boiled corn on the cob. There was no doctor here either. No pharmacy. No post office. There was no mailbox. No kiosk too.

"Dear God, we are left to fend for ourselves here!" My friend was clutching her head, distraught. By the end of the summer, she went to the beach five times, five minutes at a time. She is an incredibly good woman, but rigid, too disciplined.

"What are we going to eat?" she would lament.

"We'll fish, babe. What are you worried about? Look, there's plenty of fish. Here, one of them has just bitten me," Jovan replied.

The babe was crying.

Jovan came out of the water, threw his goggles and snorkel, realized that he ate shit, hugged Jasna, and cozied up to her.

We found a dingy shop, a combination of the butcher's and bakery. It was not opened when it rained. It was not open when it was about to rain either (the wind is blowing, the sun had set behind the clouds).

"Who is the owner?" we thought. What a jerk!

The jerk was an adorable young man whose parents felt he needed to be taught what it was like to work and make money. The adorable young man loved an easy life and, if he could, get women who suit such a lifestyle. One evening, while he was chopping steak meat with a cleaver, he invited me for a drink (you can't know if you don't try).

"Momcilo, what should I do, that man is a source of our food... And he has a cleaver." I nodded in Jovan's direction.

"Let go, bestie, don't be a party pooper, at least he's young. Imagine if he were an old man," Jovan chimed in.

"He wouldn't have invited you over if he knew about Momcilo," Jasna was predictable.

"Young, sweet, he offers meat in exchange for having a drink with me... It's worth the sacrifice, but Momcilo ... What shall I tell him?"

Cile, whom we completely forgot about but who did not forget us, opened his blue eyes wide and said sharply, "Well, be straight with him and tell him the truth—'I would, gladly, but you see, I'm married.'"

Ivana, the mother of another of Cile's schoolmates, recently complained to me:

"My child was interested in what I did for fun as a girl. I told her— your mom went to an Esperanto course, was an active mountaineer, camped all over Europe. When she asked me why I stopped doing all of that I too was shocked with the answer I gave her: "I got married." I wanted to strip down naked, go out on the terrace and scream, I swear to God!"

Why do people get married, divorced, cheat?

I thought of the unfortunate Madame Bovary and the over-the-top trial of Gustave Flaubert.

When the judge insisted on Flaubert answering who Madame Bovary was, he thundered from the defense dock:

"Madame Bovary, that's me!"

Cile shouts from the kitchen:

"Can I have another ice cream?"

"No."

"I'll have it anyway."

"Then why are you even asking me?"

"So, you don't accuse me later of not asking you."

I like to walk with Cile. We have great conversations on our walks. Cile presents me with a dilemma:

"I don't know if I'll be a rapper or a sharpshooter when I grow up."

Fifty Cent vs Vasily Zajtsev (world famous Soviet sniper during World War II).

"You can be both. Fans can come to your concert, and then you practice shooting at them."

We are laughing. We arrive at the fountain in the town center. Cile squints, makes a wish, throws coins into the fountain. He rubs his hands. He did a good job.

"What did you wish for?"

"For our soccer team to become world champions."

There is a huge tumble in our building. Phones are ringing, intercoms too, neighbors are scuttling, running around in the hallways.

It all started about a month or two ago, when the head of our building council, Nada, issued the following decree: "Building tenants are invited to donate a certain amount of money because we desperately need new keys for the bicycle shed."

For the umptieth time.

To avoid close contact with her, we all unanimously agreed with her request, whether or not we stored our bicycles in the shed.

Everyone except Lepa. Lepa and Nada can't stand each other. And they were good friends until their daughters got into a fight. The rift was over unidentified men. Apparently, one has been having various lovers over in her apartment, while another one specialized in fiancés.

Regardless.... The key was made even without Lepa's money. Lepa made a duplicate (Nada is still looking for a mole), and she regularly left her bike in the bike shed.

Today, her bike disappeared. Lepa suspects it's Nada's doing. Nada accuses Lepa. They are running wild around the building, looking for allies. They rang my doorbell too. I turned down the music. I was not home. Bob Dylan and I just popped out.

It's 1 a.m. I get a message from Nadja:

"Are you sleeping or writing?"

After the initial disapproval, my friends were obsessed with the idea of me writing the letter. Especially Nadja.

"I'm not sleeping," I reply. I can't tell her I'm not even writing at the moment. She would disown me.

Nadja needs this letter. And Sonja too. And a few more people. I'm only hesitating about you, James. You need it too, there's no point in... splitting hairs now...

Not to mention that everybody needs James Dean!

Everyone is participating, something is happening. They shower me with advice:

"Be honest, that's all."

"Don't suck up to him."

"Honest, but careful."

"You can do whatever you want, he doesn't know you anyway."

What should I do, James, how should I proceed? Everybody has a different opinion about that.

I hope it won't be "too many cooks spoiled the broth."

Although, hearing that I could do whatever I wanted calmed me down a bit.

Should I fake it? Pretend?

Like my father's cousin, Desa, who couldn't even pee without having her makeup on. She usually answered her phone in "opera" voice:

"Helloooo? ... Ah, it's only you, Mile! Go to hell!"

Or should I spill out everything that's on my mind so you can deal with it, James?

Aarrgh! This letter is driving me crazy.

"When you go crazy, no one will even notice," Bata muses again.

"Is it too late to call you?" Nadja continues the message.

"It's never too late."

It's half past one. The two of us are chatting.

Momcilo staggers from the bedroom:

"Do you know what time it is? Who are you talking to?"

"With James, who else would I be talking to?"

We giggle like teenage girls. Momcilo rolls his eyes.

Nadja lives in Sremska Mitrovica. She founded a children's theater with her friends, creates beautiful plays and travels around Serbia. It always comes as a surprise to her to see how her small community's children are so uncorrupted compared to the city ones.

She has been dating Mario for years. They have been breaking up and reconciling for years, as the seasons change. Nadja pulls the strings.

Winter is starting and she is preparing for the trip to Cyprus, where she lived as a young girl. She hates winter, the slush, Serbia, Mario. "Don't even get me started." Mario goes fishing. At the break of dawn, Nadja unpacks the suitcases she tripped over in the hallway of her house. Mario's boat docks. They came back. Each from their own trip, brimming with nostalgia and impressions.

Mario is a professional photographer. He has an eye for hidden, ordinary details.

"Well, we haven't seen this one, it's so beautiful!" is the most common comment heard at his photo-exhibition.

Milan introduced me to Nadja and Mario; they were his friends in the beginning. One summer, they stumbled upon the Valley, bought a cottage next to Dad's, and all three found themselves on the same path of festivity, marked by a strong friendship.

Mario often recounts how Milan caught a huge carp.

The fish struggled, twisting the fishing rod, dragging it to the bottom, jumping out of the water, twisting and turning, slapping on the water. The fishing rod ended up under the boat. Milan cursed, got up and grabbed the thick fishing nylon with his hands. He pulled out the carp, held it tightly, looked at it, cursed once more and released it into the Danube ("because he is a fighter"). He then washed his bloody hands in the water, turned the boat around and went home.

PLEASE DO NOT SPIT ON THE FACADE
Huge sign in Laza Telecki Street.
Some guys stop by, read it, laugh and move on.
After a few steps, one comes back, and spits on it:
"Fuck them, it's such an eyesore!"

My lungs are on fire. I smoke a packet a day again. During one of my hypochondriac episodes, I rush to see my acquaintance, a radiologist. He does an X-ray of my lungs. They are clean. I leave his office and light a cigarette in the street.

Cile has been pestering me for days:

"Buy me a parrot, I want a parrot, everyone has a parrot...!"

I find out that 'everyone' is just Stefan.

"Cile, he will be lonely in a cage, without friends," I say.

"All parrots are lonely," he replies.

I dreamed of lonely rainbow-colored parrots all night. They played with fans, plush toys, mirrors and bells in their cages...

As of this morning, Rambo the Parrot is a full-fledged member of our family.

Cile gave me an offer I couldn't refuse:

"Either you get me a parrot or a brother. OK, a sister would do too."

B. F. F.

What is that? Guess!

B. F. F. I read it on Cile's Facebook profile. Posted by his friend Mia.

"B. F. F." Cile answers.

What are they whispering to each other? What is that all about? Should I ask him?

Omerta at work.

"I told you he was too young to be on Facebook..." Momcilo objects. Ivana, Mia's mom, finally reveals the secret:

BEST FRIENDS FOREVER.

Momcilo comes home from work. I am reading your poems.

"Is there any dough to eat?" he asks.

There is something seriously wrong with this man. Cile is with Nemanja at a soccer match. I'm on a diet. And right now I'm getting all mushy over some verses.

There is no dough or bread, the kitchen is closed, it's a fasting period, there is no "dough" for you here today, but I would like to read you a poem, do you want to?

I didn't tell him any of that. I put the book away, I dragged myself to the kitchen and made him spaghetti.

Momcilo used to call me "pumpkin" and now I'm his pumpkin pie ("So what?! Pumpkin pie is really juicy and delicious, I'm a pumpkin pie fan").

Ana's outburst, which was the talk of the town for a long time, came to mind recently.

She and Ivan were freshly married, Olja was just born. Ivan's parents came to visit every day to check on Olja's progress and to gauge how well their daughter-in-law is handling everything. I stopped by her place briefly, bought her cigarettes, kissed the baby. Ana, Olja, and I were sitting on one side of the room, her father- and mother-in-law on the other. Ivan comes, washes his hands, changes into a tracksuit, sways into the kitchen. He returns quickly and sits next to his mama.

"What's there to eat?" he asks.

"I put everything in the fridge. There is a small pot and a bowl with salad. It just needs to be warmed up," Ana instructs him.

"So warm it up."

"Come on, Ivan! Can't you do it by yourself?"

"I can. But I want you to give me something to eat."

"Well, why don't you just say so." Ana stands up, unbuttons her blouse, takes out one breast swollen with milk and shoves it right under his nose:

"Here you go! That's the only way I can get you to eat!"

You don't have to fight for me
Although
You don't have to save me from a sinking ship
Or take me out of the wreckage of a burning plane
Wash the dishes
Sometimes

Momcilo works a lot. He is one of the bosses in one of the big state companies and assistant professor at the college.

Until two years ago, I had three shops. I sold books, CDs, perfumes, toys, cigarettes, juices, alcoholic beverages. Or rather... It would be more accurate to say that the shops owned me. I was a grateful government employee and I paid them handsomely for my work, and the opportunity provided. After a few years of stumbling, I was no longer so enthusiastic (someone needs eons, someone always stays stupid!). I sold my kidneys, paid off all my debts, locked up my business and went home to lick my wounds.

"You're not that kind of player, my boy, some people are, but you are not one of them," Milan said behind a cloud of smoke.

"How can I play when my legs are chained, I'm thrown into the quicksand full of cannibals, who can play such a game, what kind of game is that?"

"The game is as old as the Earth, and it will last as long, some people know how to play it, you don't, take it as it is and focus on other things," he blew out a little more smoke.

He went on my nerves when he was right.

Rock and roll
Rock and folk
Rock and falsh
Rock and faul
Rock and fuck

I have several interesting stories from that period to tell you.
Ready for two of them?
First story:
I am in my shop, with my new employee. It's January, Saturday morning. There isn't a single soul around. I show her how prices are levelled. I put my purse and cell phone on the counter, next to the cash register. The door slams open, a young man with a sunken face runs in, grabs my purse, and runs out.

I run after him, just seconds behind. I'm flying. I stumble on the ice, twist my ankle, don't feel pain, don't stop. I am howling. He runs away, the bag's belt swings left and right, he is holding the bag tightly with his right hand. The scenes from a series I watched on Explorer run through my head. When you are running after a criminal it is advisable to throw a hard object at him, which will knock him or slow him down. I would only slow myself down if I stop to take off my boot.

The thug picks narrow side streets.

Just like in American movies, a police car on a regular patrol appears, first they heard me, then they saw him, they later told me.

They speed up, come parallel with the thug, open the window, extend their arms, the tires squeak, they brake abruptly, grab him by his hair, and knock his head on the vehicle. He falls into the snow and mud. Two police officers get out of the car, and I run over, bending down to get my purse. The younger one stops me:

"Dear girl, don't do that. We know where we can hit and not leave a mark." After practical presentation of their "skills" they throw him in the car. I sit on the front seat with them, and we drive to the police station. They are kind and cracking jokes with me.

I am seen by a strikingly handsome inspector. He takes my information and statement, checks the contents of the bag, nothing is missing, yes, yes. I feel pain in my injured ankle, my head is spinning, I ask him to show me where the toilet is.

"Bring your purse, don't leave it like that," he says softly.

In an informal conversation, he fills me in with more details. They cannot keep the thug locked in. Jails are full. I didn't have enough money in my purse to warrant filing criminal charges, but since this was a brazen theft, criminal charges will definitely be filed. He checked. The thug has a thick criminal file, but he will remain free.

I can't believe it. He's going to rob someone else today!

"Dear lady, we do not write the laws. Unfortunately. We don't like it any more than you do. Our hands are tied. We meet with scum like him every day ... Do you have any idea how little we are paid?"

I was summoned by the court as a witness several times.

The thief was caught with my property in his hands. By the police. He confessed to the theft.

Correct?

"All correct..." The judge smiled wearily, saying the words slowly, as if addressing a mental patient. "As it is indisputable that the accused was under the influence of psychochemical substances at the time of his testimony, his confession is not valid."

Second story:

I am at my shop again, dusting the shelves and sorting out the books. I see a black jeep through the shop window. Two guys park it in front of the sidewalk. They enter the shop. Their buff bodies with short haircuts are streaked with tattoos and heavy white gold as they are buying whiskey, expensive cigarettes, being kind and joking with me.

There is commotion in the street. We get stuck at the door.

Through an open window, some bugger grabs a small black bag from the seat of their SUV. Passersby see it, pointing fingers at him, yelling.

The lowlife runs, the bag opens, bundles of Euro and dollar bank-notes fly out of it. The buff guys catch him in three jumps, lifts him off the ground, takes him to the SUV. They open the trunk and put him inside:

"Let's go for a ride to Fruska Gora," (a mountain near Novi Sad). they tell him as they gently close the trunk, get in the car, and leave.

I get a message from Sonja:

"Josip Lisac's concert has not been canceled, but now I can't get to Nis on time. I stayed home."

There was talk that Sonja and Petar would come visit us for the weekend. She wasn't so sure because of the concert but when she heard that it was canceled because of the rain, it was too late to go anywhere and letting me know the outcome of this conundrum.

"There's a good movie tonight at 11 p.m.—*Miller's Crossing*, watch it," I give her another option.

"I heard it's good. Someone told me about it, action and comedy. If I don't fall asleep we will be together—in the movie" she replies.

"You, me, and Gabriel Byrne... like you would be able to sleep."
"I'm in the mood." I am listening to John Lee Hooker and my mood is much better. Here's the maestro singing about it. It adds colors to my gray morning.

Neither painting, nor literature, nor film, have such an all-encompassing power to unite people as music.

7

Nemanja got Cile Krasic's soccer jersey, from the time when he was still playing for FC Vojvodina. Cile now trains karate. We took him out of soccer when the ball knocked out his teeth for the second time. Milk teeth, fortunately.

He didn't complain. Nor did the coach. It didn't matter much to him who would win. Cile was more of a showman, he entertained parents by imitating soccer stars and toyed around with soccer.

He told his friends:

"I'm not a good soccer player, so the coach put me as the goalkeeper."

"So, what kind of goalkeeper are you?"

"Pretty bad."

OK, he's not that good at dribbling, but he shoots the ball behind our building and cheers for our team at important matches. Cile and football are safer without each other.

Krasic's jersey is Krasic's jersey, the golden fleece, first Cile wore it instead of pajamas, then changed his mind and out of precaution took it off "not to wrinkle it," laid the jersey gently on his pillow and stared at it in love.

He got up for school quick as flash, didn't want breakfast, brushed his teeth, packed his school bag, and put the jersey on. It was down to his knees.

"Cile, the jersey is too big, we'll hang it on your wall, you can wear it later."

"Whaaaaaaa...Today is the worst day of my life! Whaaaaaaa!!"

He is wailing so much that we can see the state of his tonsils.

And an abundantly clear drama that is unfolding.

"Okay, you can wear your jersey, go, rinse your face. YOU CAN GO TO SCHOOL IN YOUR JERSEY!"

He didn't hear us the first time.

Suddenly, there's no trace of sadness except for the few red dots on his little face.

He is proudly sticking his chest out in front of the mirror, today, he will be the cool one at school, and it even seems that he's grown a little in Krasic's jersey.

I'm laughing, I have to tell you, Jamie.

In the sports hall, next to the gym where Cile trains karate, there is a small boxing gym.

A picture of Sylvester Stallone as Rocky can be seen through the open door, you can smell the sweat, but fresh one, so to speak, the smell of fighting, you can hear the blunt sound of the kicks on the boxing bag.

I like these young guys, future boxers, daring and robust.

An older muscular man with a broken nose, whom I suppose is their coach, has never once failed to comment with obvious contempt on a procession of little karate players, tightly wrapped in white kimonos.

As soon as he sees them passing by, he runs in front of them, tears their belts:

"Come on! Take off those pajamas, kids! They're only tripping you up!. They're for girls, ballerinas... Take them off! You're making yourself look like.... mama's boys!"

I went to pay the bills. Phone, power, cable.

The air is moist, I am in a hurry and sweating beyond measure. I imagine a cold Coke. I get to the small post office—it's closed! I go to the bank, and after waiting in line for ten minutes, for the clerk to recite to me in a deadpan voice:

"We do not accept payments after 12 o'clock."

"Why?"

"Only the bank's clients can make payments on Saturdays."

"What would happen if you processes this payment?"

She's quiet and blinks. Everyone wants to go home.

I have no other option but to go to the main Post Office in the town center. Did I already say that I am in a hurry?

Horror! I'm covered in sweat. The pavement is melting.

The main Post Office is crowded. Today, everyone has decided to pay their bills.

A young pregnant woman is standing in the middle of the row, blowing her nose into a handkerchief. Both in front and behind her are all men. An older woman is standing next to me. I am finding it hard to restrain myself.

"Is it possible that none of you will let this woman cut the line? Look at her belly—she will give birth at this post office. And you, the future mother..." I now growl at the pregnant woman, "Why are you just standing there, picking your nose? Can't you see the sign—PREGNANT WOMEN FIRST SERVED?"

Nobody gets what's going on. The attack was unexpected.

The older woman next to me smiles and tugs at my sleeve. She breaks the silence:

"My niece is pregnant. She is so happy. It's indescribable. No, no. I have never seen anyone so happy."

An uptight hat-wearing gentleman looks me straight in the eye. He's angry, doesn't like being called out. He looks like a retired teacher. I can see that he is considering whether to engage in verbal conflict.

He adjusts his glasses. His hat is shaking.

I expect an outburst of anger.

The pregnant lady cuts the line and withdraws money at the counter. He notices that:

"All is well that climaxes well. We are all happy now."

He snuffles.

In an instant, it all becomes very comical to me: his comment, my nervousness, the woman who wouldn't shut up about her pregnant niece, all that confusion. I start laughing out loud. Somebody else starts laughing too. We are all laughing now, wholeheartedly. This laughter is something that we are all sharing together, at that moment, in the dusty post office. The older lady laughs too, but she didn't catch the right moment so she is laughing at something else. Which doesn't matter...

Sun rays are hitting the clouds
The glittering yellow
The wind sings in the trees
Spreads the seeds
Waters shapes rocks
Nature creates for her own sake
We create
Red letters

Have you read Jack London's story, "The Pagan"? Such a timeless writer, a great story.

When my Granny broke her hip and was housebound for a while, she sent me on a mission. I had to go to church every week and quietly, unobtrusively collect the latest gossip.

I wasn't quite up to the task but had a strong desire to achieve the goal. I snuck between the incense burners and the benches. Undercover. Local "hens" were more preying on me than I was on them, but occasionally I did manage to smuggle a few "warm eggs."

Which were "rotten." Granny was not satisfied.

Those who persist win.

It's almost noon. It's warm. The air in the church is stuffy. We are all tranced by the heat and the pastor's monotonous chanting.

"God have mercy," he chants as we all make the sign of the cross, accompanied by endless mumbling. Here comes another chant—"God have mercy"—and we are making the sign of the cross again.

The pastor is in raptures. He has a blissful expression on his face, the same as when he was eyeing up my Granny's famous Pazin turkeys.

"God have mercy," we are making the sign of the cross.

VROOM!

This sound is definitely not coming from the pastor, let alone from the Almighty.

VROOM! VROOOOM!

The rumbling noise is getting stronger.

Aunt Mara is making the sign of the cross yet again. Just in case.

The deacon rushes outside. He comes back quickly and whispers in pastor's ear.

The pastor's eyes widen. He tilts his head back. Some kind of hat he is wearing falls off...I don't know what it is called since there are so many different types of these things for different purposes, it's a hat of some sort. He picks up a large heavy book from which he was reading and slams it on the rickety table with all his might.

"I damn anyone," he hollers, "who drives a tractor by the church on Sunday."

His dark hair flutters, whipping across his face. His eyes are shining and are pointed toward the ceiling, covered in paintings of saints. Silent, but the only worthy witnesses of his humiliation and crusade.

"Let all their fruit dry up. Let everything they sow rot!"

Pages are flying from the already worn-out book, the legs of the altar are threatening to give way.

The wide black sleeves of his robe swing across the church like wild ravens. Only a red beak-like nose shines on his deathly pale face. His voice gets hoarse from the yelling and he starts coughing.

Maybe he'll throw up?

The tractor driver is still driving around carefree. He has no idea what kind of force he had insulted, and that all his efforts have been in vain. Poor thing.

Once the priest depleted all his energy, hatless, with a distorted face, he stares at everyone present. We are to blame too.

Aunt Mara got the brunt of it:

"No communion for you, Mrs. Mara, today!" No blessing. Maybe because she was baptized when she shouldn't be?

He didn't say anything to me, and I got the communion.

In the case of this pastor, I think it's because I have big breasts.

That day I took a real golden egg to my Granny.

Scarlet letters
Gold letters
Wailing Wall
The Wall of Silence
The dead
Those who died
In Your name

For Your deeds
We crucify You

8

Jamie!

Our horrible green parrot Rambo tore up my poem!

He chewed, crushed, and destroyed an entire page!

He flaps his wings ostentatiously and covers the remaining paper noodles with shit.

I don't believe in omens (it's no good being superstitious because it's bad luck), but I can't help but wonder—maybe this letter is better suited for a bottle? I would roll it nicely, push it into the bottle, throw it into the river... Let it find its way! Let it float. Search for the mainland. Solid ground.

I don't even believe in floating.

I'd rather put the little asshole in the bottle.

I am cleaning his cage, he's talking to me, I am talking to him, but we don't really understand each other. He tilts his head, looks at me, and pecks my hand once and once again.

The green puffy blabbermouth.

Jimmy boy.

Cowboy.

I enjoy watching old westerns, Jimmy. Even though I can't help but choke with laughter when I see John Wayne's walk that defies the laws of gravity.

As a child, I would nestle into my dad's lap while nibbling on fried sprats and without hesitation, breathlessly cheered for the good guys.

That was easy. We knew who the good guys were, and even better, the good guys always won.

Everything unfolded clean, easy, and fast.

The villains were pushing up the daisies, the quack doctors were covered in tar and feathers, the gentle girls ended up in the arms of their saviors, and the sheriff's badge brings the law into the town.

I'm not sure who the good guys are today, Jimmy-boy. Not where they are. We need them. Urgently. Alive.

You do know that I am promoting you everywhere, James? I talk about your books. I lent Sonja one. Reluctantly.

As she reads on, she sends me messages full of praise:

"He knows how to write. He's amazing. Thanks."

"Watch out, step back a little, this doesn't make any sense, I give you a book to have fun, and you stab with a knife in the back," I tease her.

"If it is a knife, it's plastic," she justifies herself.

"A knife is a knife," I shoot back.

That sentence reminded me of another of Milan's stories.

His friend got a job as a night watchman. This was an extremely thin man who didn't care about food. He ate so he wouldn't die.

Night shifts have inexplicably changed his view of food.

Before going to work, he bought enormous quantities of groceries. A few loaves of bread, salami, sausages, garlic, black onions, cheese, bacon. He wouldn't even taste any of it, but he refused to move without his bundle.

To all questions, requests, pleas in search of the reason for such insane behavior, he answered briefly and (un)clearly:

"Night is night."

Otherwise calm and reasonable, he confused everybody even more with his persistent repetition of this ritual, not deviating one iota:

"I already told you and I can only repeat it—night is night."

The night watchman knew something the others didn't.

Everything I write to you does not necessarily express my views, James. Night is night.

I am driving Cile to school. It's 7.15 a.m. We are late. It's not raining, it's as if the Niagara Falls are crashing directly on my car. I am driving from memory, one windshield wiper works halfway and the windshield heater is broken.

"And what are we going to tell the teacher, why are we late?" Cile asks.

"You know the reason. You were learning that poem by heart until only five minutes ago," I answer.

"I don't want to tell him that."

Look at this lunatic, turning without signal!

"Do you have a suggestion?" I ask him.

"Shall we say you didn't hear the clock?"

"So, it's my fault now?"

"It's not your fault if you didn't hear the clock."

I give up. The clock is to blame.

The engine coughs, the car jerks and stops. I'm pumping the gas pedal. Nothing. Dead. No! No! I refuse to accept this. No gas. There is a gas station nearby, thank heavens.

With a greasy gallon gas can in my hands, I make my way through the rain.

"GAS STATION CLOSED. DETANKING IN PROGRESS," a hated sign is mocking me.

The heavens are snoring.

An unknown man waves his arms like a windmill, saying something. Fool. I ignore him. He approaches me, still swirling his hands. Well, this is the straw that broke the camel's back!

"What do you want from me, what's wrong with you, man?"

"You blocked me, move your car, I'm late!"

Together we push the car a few meters away.

I'm calling a taxi from my cell phone.

♪♫"... If you're cool, you'll ride with us... ♪♫, "We have no available vehicles, ma'am. I am sorry."

I am sorry too.

Second, third, fifth call. I'm shooting blanks. I call the first taxi company again.

♪♫"... We're always here for you. If you're cool...♪"Then, I hear a live person's voice and explain my dilemma.

"The taxi will be with you in five minutes."

I am waking up Cile again:

"Is the taxi coming?"

"It is," I hope and pray.

In the taxi, Cile remembers that he left his school bag in our car.

I will go crazy! I really will.

There's the excuse.

I am going to postpone the madness for another time. I opt for the clock version. It is the shortest.

At last. Cile is at school. His feet are wet. I hope he doesn't catch a cold. I light a cigarette, inhale the smoke or two, and throw it into the ocean in which I'm...drowning.

I call the taxi again and I manage to get one in the first attempt.

"Ma'am, didn't I drive you a little while ago?" A shrewd taxi driver.

"Please, just keep quiet and pretend not to notice me."

He drives me to my car to get the gallon can, then to the gas station and back to the car.

I unlock the door of my apartment, I'm schlepping to the bathroom to take off my wet clothes. I'm sneezing.

I glance at my watch. It's not even 9 o'clock. I was convinced that it was close to 11 and that I should go and pick up Cile from school immediately. I forgot I didn't have breakfast. It's too late for breakfast and too early for lunch.

I can't keep up with the times. The clock is to blame.

9

Momcilo annoys me.

And his walk. He's strutting around in his underpants, leaving his pubes behind him. And his silence. And his talking. And his ugly glasses that look hideous on him.

It has nothing to do with you, James. It has nothing to do with Momcilo either.

The links are broken in my case.

I don't understand what he's telling me. Probably:

"Why don't you sit here in the armchair?"

I am standing on the terrace, propped up on my elbows, smoking.

"I'm on the terrace, smoking."

"I know. Why don't you sit here? In the armchair?"

I read him my poem, at his urging. He is focused, listens carefully.

"How do you like it?"

"Which of the two?"

Maybe he's doing it on purpose. A thought that makes it a little easier for me.

"It's because you see each other only for a short time. You don't have time to get used to it, the children asked me this morning if Daddy comes home at all, he leaves at 6 and comes back at midnight," says Ana.

"How do we get used to that when he comes home only to take a shower and change clothes?"

"What would you like? Some bastard sleeping with his face covered by the newspaper? They are hunters, and hunting takes time..."

How, how?

"Strong hunters ..."

"They can't always bring home a bear... or... a bison. Sometimes a bison, sometimes.. a groundhog..." Ana is relentless.

We are their only catch. Trophies that dust.
Drought demons
Rule
Beasts circling
Dusty watering holes
Digging Clawing
Scraping Roaring
Seeking Source of
Water
Blood
Tears
Semen

When Momcilo and I wanted to spice up our sex life, we went into one of the bookstores in Zmaj Jovina Street. Armed with a bulky picture book, we hurried home, opened it on the bed, and threw ourselves into studying.

"Well, we know this ... And we tried this ... Whoaaa, we discovered this ages ago!"

Is this a biology textbook for the seventh grade?

"Go on, continue flipping through it, that's the beginning, maybe in the middle..."

The majority is in the middle.

We both knew the end.

We threw the book under the bed, and we spread out on it.

Our bed lacked nothing. Except for the two of us.

I am doing everything I can, I swear. I polish shoes. I scrub the tiles behind the washing machine. Nothing helps.

"Cile, turn off the computer, let's go for a ride to the dog Shelter!"

Cile is crazy about dogs. I'm crazy for taking him.

"Can we...?" we haven't even left yet, and he starts.

"No, we can't. No pups, no sick dogs, no 'awww, look how he's look-ing at me' dogs." He must learn when to stop.

"Mom, can Aleksandar come with us?"

The dog shelter was founded by Zorica, a woman I read about in a newspaper article. It is located behind the town of Budisava, to the left of the Grlić grange.

As we pass the grange, we come across a large house between two fields, surrounded by wire.

The barking, the yelping, and the squealing drown out Cile's and Aleksandar's shrieks. The two of them are deliriously happy.

In a telephone conversation, Zorica told me that we can come after five o'clock, because she feeds the dogs from four to five, and during that time they are very irritable and not up for playing.

I look at my watch. 4:18. A strong, smallish woman, must be Zorica, is looming behind the mountain of dogs. There are so many of them! They have merged into a shapeless, shaggy, wavy, screaming mass. They swamp Zorica. Her hands are sticking out, one foot in the boot, she's fine, and her head is in its place. She gestures and points to something. I understand that for now, we can walk around the field and watch the dogs behind the fence.

Cile is running far in front of me, Aleksandar is running around my legs.

Unexpectedly, as it usually happens, a werewolf, nothing else looks like it, jumps over the fence. Cile fainted with happiness.

I hurry towards him, Zorica screams:

"Squat, squat fast and don't move!"

I can already see the newspaper headlines in my head:

"A mother and two children were bitten to death by a rabid dog in a field!"

Silence. The werewolf does not bark. Doesn't even growl. He sniffs us and climbs on my back with his front paws.

I hear the sound of Zorica's footfall:

"Lady, get down! You naughty girl!"

The dogs ate their food portions, no supplements, Zorica is chatting away, and I am half-dead.

She knows every dog by their name. Patting them. Golden retrievers, cocker spaniels, Dalmatians (I almost wrote 101), German Shepherds, Dobermans, stray dogs... She finds them by the roadside, around garbage containers. Bitches are her priority. ("They just knock them up.")

"Reporters are coming, they want to interview me, take pictures of me. Why the hell do you want to take a picture of me, take a picture of this misery? Send money... How would I otherwise get by? Three business owners from Serbia and a few French and Swedes. I thank them from the bottom of my heart, but it's still not enough. These dogs eat like there's no tomorrow. What about vaccines, medicines, shampoos...?"

The villagers are the ones who are causing her problems. They set her house on fire this fall. There's no evidence to corroborate that, but she knows...

The worst person was the one that cut off Ken's front paws with a scythe.

She shows me a photo of a black puppy sleeping in a purple crib.

"Two French women, rich, lesbians, took him to Paris. They called him Kangaroo, Ken for short, because he was jumping around on his hind legs, poor thing. I photocopied his picture and put it up everywhere in Budisava. I knocked on that monster's door and said, "Here, you bastard, look how Ken lives now, in silk and velvet, and you will shit in your garden all your life. And I hope your children and grandchildren will too."

10

I moved three times, always living on the Boulevard. Farther from Futoska Market, closer to Futoska Market, across from the market.

Ever since I was a girl, I always used to meet in that area a young man with messy hair and a smile on his face.

We always somehow managed to miss each other.

He is walking on the pedestrian crossing, I'm running across the street in the middle of the road.

Me on the pedestrian crossing, he's dodging cars.

Both on the crossing, one of us on the phone.

He walking, I'm in the car.

Each time we clearly touched each other with our eyes.

Later, we smiled and waved, greeting each other.

I sent him a kiss from the car.

He's shouting in my direction:

"If I man...d... to g..t to th..."

Dozens of cars, buses, trucks grind his words.

I don't understand how we never met in the city, Novi Sad is small, everyone knows everyone. Or so they think.

We saw each other this morning too.

Messy hair, smiling from ear to ear, points to his bag with bread and yogurt, newspapers in the other hand.

Both my hands are free, I wave them in the direction of the hair salon, we laugh.

Everyone is on their side of the Boulevard.

A look
Or less
A hint
A murmur
Or more
Breath
I want
Or not
I do not know

Njegoseva Street is crowded.

A tow truck is stuck between rows of parked cars.

Sweat is pouring from the truck driver's pores, which he didn't even know he had. A large rear-view mirror was not enough for him—he threw half his body out the window, maneuvered, and moved away at a snail's pace.

Passers by slow down, stop, give conspiratorial smiles.

No one cheers for the tow truck. Unless it was Spiderman.

Well, today I did something for my body.

I exercised at the gym.

The owner is a friend of mine from elementary and high school, Sale Bronx.

Sale has a reputation as a "tough guy." When he speaks, his reputation greatly surpasses him. Of course, it depends on the interlocutor.

He has a short fuse and it doesn't take much to set him off into a punching match.

It's late in the evening, the Corral Cafe is chock full, we are breathing down each other's necks. A group of drunken rude people are hitting on us. The loudest among them spills beer on Lena's shirt. He grits his teeth, thinks he's funny. We can't all think the same. Sale thumps the guy's head on the table.

"How about you pick your teeth with broken fingers, huh, you ape?!"

Blood splatters across Lena's shirt which now takes on red tones.

The ape leaves with the rest of the pack, collides with the door, but not because of the beer.

Sale takes off his shirt:

"Put this on, I'm sorry, I didn't mean it," he says to the girl who is dead pale in the face.

Sale and Lena are now married, they have a daughter, have invested a lot in the gym and their business is doing well.

"Where are you, dude?" I greet him.

"I'm always here for you. Whatever you need," he replies.

"I want you to make me prettier, younger, and ... and ..."

What else? My brain suddenly stops, I'm dumb even when it comes to my wishes.

"A silent, deadly chick," Sale continues.

He almost guessed it right. Has an idea to spare.

"Get on the bike, for starters," he says.

I relentlessly turn the pedals as if my life depends on it and imagine rude guys, whistling and howling at me.

"What did you say? Did you say something to me?"

"I'm telling you for the tenth time," Sale stands in front of me, grabbing the helm.

"Get off the bike, your muscles will get sore. That's enough for today!"

Nemanja has a girlfriend. "A real girlfriend," to quote Cile.

He drenched his hair with styling gel. Even Italian gigolos would envy him. He spritzed a whole bottle of perfume onto himself, while breaking another one earlier. A bunch of colorful belts like lianas are hanging from his neck. He's struggling a lot choosing which color goes best with black pants.

Getting ready for a date. He'll never be more ready for one.

"Where are you going?" Bata asks him.

Nemanja mumbles something.

"What?" No one understood what he said.

Again, a vague answer.

"Speak up, why are you so shriveled up, where are you going?" Nemanja bursts out:

"To the theater! THE-A-TER!!"

Bata gets up from the armchair, he gets in Nemanja's face:

"To the theat... Theater?!... Hey, my son..." He sighs, shakes his head:

"You've reached the bottom of the barrel, son, the very bottom, you can't get any lower than this..."

"And after that you'll have dinner at Jovana's mom's," Isidora adds fuel to the fire.

Bata clutches his chest and stumbles back into the chair:

"You want them to laugh at us, to point a finger at me—my only son! To the theater.. Son, tell Daddy who won—LA Lakers or Dallas Mavericks? There, he doesn't know... They put a spell on him, what else could it be... he's finished..."

Nemanja turns in disgust and runs away.

"You're shooting yourself in the foot, my son. In the foot!"

Bata's voice echoes down the hall.

Flower in a cactus. Isidora.

A grumpy high school girl, as one should be when in puberty.

"Dora seems to have leaped from teething to her hormones raging. Others are getting destroyed by them," Sandra often says.

Isidora finishes every sentence in a high-pitched voice. Her sentences are declarative.

She refuses to be like a Barbie doll, hats are in fashion. Dora wears a baseball cap, artificial nails, cuts her natural nails so short they bleed, refuses to go out with airheads who think of suntanning and plucking their eyebrows as the highlight of their day!

"Let me do your hair ... Be like a girl, look, hairpins ... Isidora!"

Her friends already have boyfriends.

Isidora loves horses. Bata's friend has a farm in Cenej, she spends rainy and sunny days there, grooming, feeding, and riding them.

I cheer for Dora and don't worry about Dora. A cowboy will ride into town, the original, at the right time and find his way to her. She will know how to recognize him. Because she is unique too.

"You look like two limp horses. Can't you see that something is going on with your daughter?!" the aunt is always in a gung-ho state.

Full alert.

Cile has diarrhea:

"What did you do to the child?!"

Just before we're leaving for the summer vacation:

"Take care of the child, call me, and... don't go too far into... fucking sea!"

Momcilo, Cile and I are riding on a moped. We are driving to the Olympus.

"I don't want to be in a sandwich!" Cile wants to be the driver.

There are no signposts. It seems that the Olympus is still far away. There is no one around. Momcilo is driving, there are flies and bugs getting into our eyes and mouths. Momcilo is still driving. In the distance we hear thunder and see occasional lightning strikes. The engine stops, we are poisoned by exhaust fumes, our legs are massacred by flies and bugs. We are surrounded by "no photos" signs. No wonder, because these are NATO bases.

My knees are trembling.

"Don't go too far," my aunt's sinister words are echoing in my head.

I am reading poems I wrote about twenty years ago. (It's been that long?)

The themes are uniform.

Immortal love, pledges, suffering, which all lead to the meaninglessness of an already cruel life.

Dear God, who did I write all this for?

I rummage through my memory. It's dark.

I didn't forget Ljubisa.

Most of my boyfriends didn't have a clue about their role, and therefore knew nothing about the torment and misery that these bastards inflicted on me. All the adventures began and ended in my notebooks.

Ljubisa did end up in my notebook, but that was preceded by a lovely and exciting period of dating.

He was 28, I just turned 19.

He was the first man that made me orgasm. I read Serbian writer and expressionist Crnjanski with him. He was a painter. A good one, actually one of the better painters according to critics and "colleagues" from an already established milieu. He did not care much for public acceptance, I was hellbent on proving that students in Serbia take a long time to graduate.

We spent days driving in his Ford across Vojvodina.

We chose overgrown side roads, stopping when a landscape touched us. And to pee.

For him, everything was a painting. For me, everything was words.

On one of these wanderings we came across a gray puppy with tangled hair.

Buck, that's what we called him. We cut his hair and washed him. He moved into Ljubisa's house and was our baby.

I don't remember ever knowing such a direct, spontaneous, unencumbered person as Ljubisa was.

Ljubisa was a drug addict.

He told me that one afternoon in bed, while Buck was jumping and slobbering all over us.

I cried like rain. I knew it was over.

"That was the most painless way to break up with him, my boy." Milan did not see him as a potential son-in-law.

Ljubisa went to the Netherlands and never returned.

Whenever I see some people from that time who might have news about him, I cross the street to the other side. I don't want to hear it.

I don't have the heart to not write you an old poem dedicated to him.

Falling
Stillborn
Crucified on this paper
In blood
In the foam
Naked
Words
Instead of Children
That I wanted to have with you

My friend Marina is divorced.
Milos, Momcilo's friend, is single.
And I had good intentions.
Marina and Milos lukewarmly agreed to a blind date, which more than justified its name. I was stunned.

Were the two of them in the same place on the same day? Did they meet?

Marina's side of the story:

"I don't understand men at all! We went to the Salas 84 restaurant. While we were in the car, he already started asking me questions: what kind of music do I listen to, where do I work, how old is my daughter... I felt as if I was being interrogated. "Loosen up a bit, let's fool around a bit, relax, it's a beautiful day...

"When we arrived at the restaurant, my head was pounding.

"He took to the menu like a pro, probably counting how much money it will all cost, I wasn't consulted on anything. Climate was his main and side topic. He spoke on his cell phone twice about some great business deal! Yeah, like you're a player... I didn't expect much, but... He didn't even ask me for my phone number. He's tongue-tied. And he doesn't look that bad, really..."

Milos's version of the story:

"Women don't know what they want! I wanted us to loosen up, the usual things—work, the music she likes, but she was mum! Maybe she's shy, she said she had a headache. I didn't want to bother her with the menu, and I wasn't sure what she liked. I don't even know what I ordered. I also mentioned children, to soften her up. I was rambling on about the weather, so she wouldn't think I am nobody. I even talked to Momcilo about supposedly a big business deal. Kissing her was the furthest thing from my mind, she would bite my tongue off. It is what it is, let's move on... But she is kinda cute."

Jamie, Jamie, Jamie.

This letter is getting out of control, Jamie. And I don't know who's to blame.

Gay parade is the word, Jamie.

I really couldn't care less about people being born queer, James? They won't even brush against me if I don't let them.

The other ones, who are bending over out of interest, burning their sins with candles, chanting, lamenting, ego-maniacal heroes, commissioned sages, insidious soul-saving preachers, fattened hermits...

They are fucking us, James, raping, brainwashing, sucking our guts out, making holes in our pockets. James, no one has put condoms on their tongues. James, no one has cut them short, broken their legs or at least tripped them.

Who is to blame, James? Who?

Pinky, pinky bow-bell,
Whoever tells a lie
Will sink down to the bad place,
And never rise up again.

11

The elevator.

It can hold 450 kilograms of meat and bones. Four adults, eventually five.

Some people are talkative: "Howdy, neighbor. How much did you pay for that t-shirt? Where did you buy it?"

Some are shy: "You go. I can wait."

Some reckless: "You don't mind me smoking?"

Others are grumpy: "G'morning."

Regardless of the character, the first thing everybody does is to pick their elevator corner. They take up their minuscule space and do not move. The fifth passenger is exposed, smacked right in the middle, fidgets, scuttles from left to right, straightens their clothes.

They recently caught the "Elevator Rapist." He brutalized a woman for hours.

My aunt, who is always too careful, is lecturing me:

"Natasha, have you read about that maniac, be careful, don't go into the elevator with strangers, N-E-V-E-R! Did you hear me?"

Our building is small. All the neighbors, with their immediate and extended families and friends know each other well.

I'm walking slowly towards the building, the strap on my sandals bothers me.

A young man is standing in front of the entrance. I slow down, scan him. He's still standing. Not moving. Like a doll from a shop window.

I unlock the door, he sneaks up behind me. I press the elevator button.

"Who are you visiting?" I ask.

"My brother."

I don't like the way he looks at me. Or what he looks like.

The elevator has arrived.

"You or me first?"

"Pardon?" he marvels.

"I'm not getting in the elevator with you. You or me?"

He nods in disbelief, walks away, gives me the advantage.

I exit the elevator on my floor.

I hear footsteps, panting. I turn around.

The sicko ran up the stairs from the ground to the seventh floor!

I punch him right in the neck. The key to the apartment is in my hand, extremely thick and full of protruding cracks. I shove it under his eye, grab him by the hair.

"Where is your brother, cunt, who's your brother, talk!! You wanted to terrorize me, huh, you pussy!!"

"On the sixth..." he stutters.

I am pushing him to the sixth floor.

Neighbors hear a noise and opened the door:

"Someone call 911. 911! Call 911!"

A brilliant idea, they just need to put it into action.

A big guy comes out of one apartment, I know him, a tenant from the sixth floor.

"Nebojsa!" addresses the attacker with bulging eyes.

"Neboj... What is this, what the fuck, what's...?! What is this !!"

The fart does have a brother.

He came from New Zealand the day before yesterday. He wanted to act cool.

Heating costs have gone up, Jamie.

We pay for the cameras in the town center, "City Eyes," that's what they're officially called.

Cile and I have come to the Village.

Acacia in front of our house smells.

I tear off the white flowers and put them in my mouth.

Cile is not impressed with what's going on.

"Try it, it's nice," I offer.

He chews. Frowns, spits them out.

Dodge and Hogar, two of my aunt's dogs, are jumping on us and around us like bouncy balls.

A neighbor has been drinking coffee in the summer kitchen (we call it kitchenette) for over an hour. She popped over to take the seedlings.

She finally gets up and leaves.

"What was she thinking?! Visiting at noon! She doesn't know when to leave," says the aunt as she puts soup plates down and follows the neighbor with her eyes.

Cile is enchanted by the aunt's soup. He ate at least two plates full.

"That's enough," I tell him. "You won't be able to eat the rest."

"Let the child eat, let him get full. You just eat until you are all full." Auntie is eyeing up Cile.

"He's a bit green... skinny. It's like he's lost weight?"

"So, what's new?" I ask between bites.

"What could be new?" the aunt answers, "Almost nothing... Milica is all bruised again, it hasn't been even... DON'T TOUCH THE DOGS WHILE YOU'RE EATING! DODGE, HOGAR, SHOOO!"

"They touched me first," Cile defends himself as he watches his aunt lock the dogs in another yard.

She comes back panting.

"They are just hungry, their mouths are hanging down to the ground, it takes me a while to feed them all, price of maize has gone up again..." she says.

"You don't give maze to dogs, Grandma." He addresses and sees my aunt as a grandmother, I mean, his grandmother.

"Forget the dogs, my darling. Granny is talking about chickens, they would eat me too..."

"I'm not hungry anymore" Cile gets up, knocks down a chair, and runs to the backyard.

Lunch continues. So does the story:

"That butcher beat her up again.... Thug!"

"Did the police come?"

"I lost count! He even threatened her with a fist from the police car!"

"I don't understand why she doesn't divorce."

"She's afraid of that blockhead, he's strong as a bull, and even if she did... She has no job and she would have to live off her sick mother. Two small children ... And...and ... It seems she's pregnant again."

"There's something wrong with that woman! She should abort!"

"She miscarried last time when he hit her in the stomach. Such a shame, it's not the child's fault..."

"I'm telling you, Mirjana works in a women's shelter, I can arrange ..."

"Forget about women's shelter. Bollocks! Don't be ridiculous, what can they do?"

"They can educate her, provide shelter, maybe even find a job ..."

"That's all nice, well done to them, but I ask you, what can they actually do, that's what I'm asking you," aunt raises her voice for another octave.

"And now what? He'll continue beating the shit out of her and..."

Aunt quickly interrupts me:

"This morning she told me: Auntie Dusica, I'm turning over a new leaf! I won't cry anymore, let him hit me. I won't say a word, that's what feeds him. Let him kill me, I won't even squeak. No!"

Aunt is cleaning the table and refusing my help. "You're not deft enough," she mutters as I am wandering around the yard.

"So, what's Nemanja's girlfriend like?" she asks me.

"Reticent, a sweetheart. Studies mathematics."

"Let him bring her over, so his grandmother can see her... And who are her parents?"

"How can I know?" Nemanja has to keep quiet.

Cile wants to go to Draga's, a neighbor across from the aunt's house.

"She told me she was going to have little guinea fowls. Come on, mom!" he tugs at my sleeve.

"No way!" The whip that is my aunt's voice strikes us on our legs. There's more.

Draga is a Village teacher, she wears a bun and speaks through her nose in front of others.

Her husband Drasko is the school principal. It's wine that talks from him in front of everyone. He's not picky, it's from his personal vineyard!

They have a daughter, Svetlana, a round, ruddy, precocious girl, who has never dared to take such a "demanding step as marriage," despite numerous suitors, who were all gentlemen.

They live with Draga's mother Zaga, in a two-story house with white pillars. The second floor is Drasko's handiwork. Personally!

Zaga is a small, hunched old woman, well known for creating and spreading awkward stories. She "broadcasts" them in the evening, and acts surprised with their content when she hears them in the farmers market the next morning. Zaga is also known for dying any day now. She has been dying ever since I can remember.

"I barely escaped the darkness," she describes vividly, wiping the corners of her mouth with her thumb and forefinger.

My aunt gets Cile busy with poppyseed strudels, while dragging me out to the kitchenette.

"Drasko cheated on Draga," she declares pompously. "With a school cook! The children were peeking out of the window and what a sight it was."

Pause.

"When she heard, Draga ran through the whole town to the station to throw herself in front of the train."

"Why? The train station is right in front of their noses." I ask superfluous questions.

"She was whining to the heavens." The aunt goes into details without even listening to me.

"Svetlana was waddling behind her, Zaga followed Svetlana, pulling her hair out in despair. The whole Village was shaking."

"Is she alive? What happened?"

"Of course, she's alive," the aunt waves her hand. "The railway had been overhauled for a week and the trains were not running."

An important pause.

"And? What now? What did the lofty missus say?"

"What? What can she say?" my aunt looks at me in amazement. "What's the matter with you, as if you don't know them! They're denying everything. Drasko is a saint personified." Aunt starts impersonating Draga, talking in nasal voice, "It's that whore that started everything.... Dear God!!! I ran through the Village?! And my Svetlana too?! As God is my witness...Zaga broke her glasses. Whoever saw it, let them come forward and say it. Oh, what a whore she is! Who gives a shit...? I buried myself in this god-forsaken town, shame on you all, you liars! And drunks!"

At home in Novi Sad, I am putting meat and cakes away in the fridge.

"So, what's new in Srem?" Momcilo inquires. "If there wasn't at least one good fight, no need to reply."

"There's nothing new. There are cakes. Aunt packed up a box full. Go deal with them."

I'm calling Ana on the phone:

"What's up, darling?"

"Darling" is a common term by which Ana, Tijana, Marina, and I use to address ourselves.

"Honey" is reserved for emergencies, crises, and cataclysms.

"I'm suffocating in heat and steam," she says.

"So, you're ironing!" The conclusion is self-evident.

"Well, screw it. Ivan is just piling on clothes. He changes two t-shirts a day. Olja and Jovan are competing for who will get dirtier. What are you doing?"

"I am alone. Momcilo and Cile are at the pool."

"Come over! I'll put coffee on, you have fifteen minutes."

"I'm there in ten."

A flock of birds
Flies across the sky
Their turns are magnificent
They open somber window shutters
Cheese Coca-Cola Dr Pepper Cheese
Fish Soysauce Cheese Lettuce
Cheese

I can do without quail eggs. Caviar. Forget truffles!

Leave me without cheese and you created a Zombie.

"No cheese, no cigarettes, Coca-Cola with ice and orange, hairdresser, perfume, cell phone, summer," Momcilo lists. "You need a lot to make you smile."

"Nah, one look at you is enough."

♪♫ "When I buy a scooter I will fly to you Ane, Ane..." ♪♫.

A song is playing on the radio.

I haven't heard it in a long time, I have no idea which station is playing it, Cile was fiddling with buttons.

My dad sang it when I was a little girl.

He loved to sing.

That song stopped me in my tracks.

Although Milan explained everything to me. When he got sick.

And I saw it.

One May, long time ago. Early May. The sun reigned supreme.

The Danube was surprisingly low.

I lost a baby. Unplanned. That I wanted to raise on my own.

I didn't eat, I didn't drink, I didn't shower, I didn't get out of bed.

I rotted in the city for days.

And then we went to the Valley, Milan and me.

He launched the boat. We drove for a long time, for hours, we were silent, the boat cut the river. The Danube absorbed the blue color of the sky and the green color of dense trees from kilometer-long river islands.

We docked on one of them. Milan handed me a chain to pull the boat in the shallows.

There was no one anywhere as far as we could see.

It seemed surreal. It's like we found ourselves on another planet.

Only the sky, the cries of birds, water.

I took off my sneakers and socks. Dug my feet deep into the sand.

The 'snow' from the poplars hovered silently around me.

I walked on the scattered shells with my eyes closed, they crunched under my feet. There was no wind. Everything was calm.

I stepped into the water, it was clear, fast, liked its coldness.

I squatted, in my clothes, the Danube flowed, carried me, dragged, rinsed, disobedient, strong, eternal, raised and lowered my hands, made waves, the sun performed the magic of rainbow colors with hundreds of tiny drops, spilling through the water, through the air, through me. I shouted, nothing articulate, letting my voice run wild.

I got into the boat, returned to Novi Sad. I returned to myself.

I'll never forget that day.

12

"What is rocism?" Cile asks me.

"Where did you hear that word?"

"On television, the fight against rocism."

"It's not rocism, it's racism. It's when some people think they're smarter and better than others because of their skin color, so they show that intelligence by humiliating and beating others."

Cile was taken aback.

"They must be very stupid! They don't go to school?"

"They don't even know what a school is, or to read or write, nothing. C'mon, brush your teeth, put on your pajamas and go to bed."

In bed, he puts his hands under his head, looking at comets and stars on the ceiling. He's contemplating something.

"Mom, I know how we're going to fight racists. You know, they don't know how to read or write. We will deceive them—it is not racism but rocism. That's how we are going to dupe them. Rocists are good and love people!"

Pepper Plate Watch Ball Pillow Street Computer Nasal Drops Catfish Now Don't Talk Crap Regardless Watch Out Bruises Why Chicken Bravo Bone Stickers Crumbs

Those are some of the words I uttered
Today
Yesterday
Tomorrow

I need it
Now
Not later
Immediately
Tomorrow it will be late
I unbelievably need it
Right now

13

School break has begun!

Ducklings are singing, "Today is a wonderful day for us, last day of our school. Long live, long live our school, hope it crashes and burns!"

Tanja asked me to pick up Saska's school records because of that misunderstanding about the school trip.

"It's all the fault of this little girl who answers the phone. Please, Nata, you go. I can't, I have a headache again."

"No problem, it'll just be more pointless if you don't show up. It'll look like you're scared," I say.

"What?! I have nothing to be afraid of. Why would I be afraid ...? The child gave up. Period! I'm not... a fool. Even if I killed a man, it's not a court martial. You just go and feel free to tell him that you have my permission."

I took both Cile's and Saska's school records.

I am reporting to Tanja:

"I told the teacher you weren't crazy to have to justify why she didn't go. It's not a trial, and you didn't kill a man."

"Nata... you didn't.... You said all that? You didn't...You did?"

"Why does it matter now? You gave me the green light. You're not a crazy killer."

Awkward silence for a couple of seconds.

"I'm yanking your chain, I didn't tell him anything. Don't be so hung up!"

"Yeah, I know you're yanking my chain, what's the matter with you, even if you were serious, big deal, you could've told him all that, no big deal."

My lentils burned, Jamie!

I'm pouring it into another pot, then into the toilet bowl.

I saved the ham, the main ingredient.

It's fucked up to write like this: cook, wash, iron, vacuum...

I need to think. String sentences together.

Oh, if only I were in a house with a sea view...

Glass windows cover the entire wall, a large rosewood table, manuscripts and a computer on it. There is a comfortable armchair, a small but carefully selected library above the armchair for the bards to support me, exotic plants in a room lit by an equally exotic lamp.

Noise of waves and wind.

Cile is with the governess. Momcilo is with the housekeeper, a nineteen-year-old Korean woman, and I... am creating.

Sky is the limit!

Do you like to be caressed, Jami(son)?

Every nerve in me is purring, my brain is blissfully empty, I levitate. Momcilo is caressing me. My back, arms, nape.

He doesn't do it as often as he used to, so I could enjoy it even more, he says.

Some of your songs caress me, James. Just so you know.

Luka and Cile are peers, they both attend the same school, but different grades.

Luka's mother is a tall, determined, straight-talking woman. We always have a good chat while we are waiting for the children to come out of the school or when we see each other in passing.

"Oh, hi!"

"Coming from the farmers market?" she asks.

"It's either school or the farmers market," I answer, "Yourself?"

Her face muscles contract.

"The world is full of all sorts of idiots. My blood pressure is sky high because of some bitch. I was going to my hairdresser's and she told me that a woman who didn't take care of her hair wasn't a real woman. And then she said that my hair was crying out for good treatment. I wanted to punch her teeth in, all the way to her pea-sized brain."

"Well, that's all she has—a pea-sized brain—which she doesn't even use, forget it, it's not worth it..."

"Yes, yes, I know. But it's hard, I can't always... Bye! See ya!"

When some people I know become caustic and unpleasant, I avoid them for a while.

They, on the other hand, are unable to do that.

The boulevard is crowded.

Same old story.

A line of four-wheelers stretched out like a chewing gum.

Gypsy children, like sparrows, are jumping around cars, arms outstretched.

They are so small, someone will run them over.

The group is led by an old woman, holding a girl in her arms.

The child squeezes the dirty doll and seems to be saying something to her.

She approaches the car in front of me.

Disappears in the blink of an eye, I can't see her, she's really fast and yet was limping just a minute ago!

A distraught woman comes out of the car where the old woman was standing, her face red as a tomato.

Vehicles stop.

The woman says something, starts turning in all directions, and only then do I see a girl with a doll crouching in the woman's arms.

"I asked her how she didn't feel sorry for the child, that she should be ashamed... And then she threw the child into my lap. Shame on her!"

She's explaining to everybody and nobody. Nobody!

The girl is still talking to the doll as if this whole ruse doesn't concern her.

Terribly calm, distant.

Drivers are honking, signaling with their lights, the traffic jam becomes even longer, they're impatient, it's enough.

The woman hands the girl over to someone from the group of black sparrows, returns to her car.

Everybody goes their own way.

Jamie, crazy day today.

I'm waiting for Tijana on the bench, on the boulevard, again.

That's what you do when you have a boulevard that is as long and spacious as ours.

We agreed to go for a walk.

I was running around a lot, totally unplanned. The blister on my heel burst open, unplanned, because of those strappy sandals. They are not made for walking, it suddenly dawns on me, they are more getting-out-of-the-car-going-to-the-theatre sandals. I don't have the guts to cancel Tijana. So, I'm sitting on the bench, my feet are killing me, the blister is throbbing, I'm digging into my purse, no lighter! No, no, no lighter. Maybe this is...? No, it's not. I hate getting up now, the kiosk is across the street. Somehow, I manage to drag myself over. "INVENTORY" the sign says conspicuously, back to the bench.

I came early, and I know that Tijana will be late, as usual.

I focus on passersby, assess which of them is a smoker, has a pleasant face, is willing to help.

"Excuse me, please, do you maybe have a lighter?"

The two smiling girls don't have one. So they say.

I decide not to approach an older woman, a young mother with a baby in a stroller and a cocky young man with a pit bull.

A woman in her late fifties, youthfully dressed, with a cheerful glint in her eye, passes by. Worth a try!

"Ma'am, please, do you have a lighter?"

I take a cigarette out of the pack, visually confirming the question.

She approaches my bench, takes the bag off her shoulders. Ha!

"I don't have a lighter, I'm sorry. I need one too and there's no kiosk in sight. Can I have a cigarette until I get to a shopping mall? If that's not a problem. Two?"

I gave her three cigarettes. I do not know why. I feel silly. I should be annoyed by that woman and I try my best to be, but I find it funny.

My attention is drawn to a middle-aged man. He seems decent. Even if he were a smelly freak, I wouldn't care. I'd ignore it. He's holding a lighter in his hand and brings its magnificent flame close to the cigarette.

"Excuse me," I've never apologized so much in my life, "can I borrow your lighter?"

"Of course! It's my pleasure," he says and adds that I can keep it. He looks at me and likes what he sees. He's not pushy or rude. I give him his lighter back.

"Thank you very much, you're very kind." I really mean it.

"You're welcome. Really, thank YOU very much," he replies.

I find that funny again.

People have gone bananas. Totally.

I once mistakenly waved goodbye to someone thinking I knew them.

And since then
From time to time
I wave
To a woman carrying garbage
Children on the playground
Old women on a bench
Girls in front of a clothes stores
Some wave back
Others don't
There are more of the latter ones
They turn around
Wondering
Shrug their shoulders

Dragomir, our next-door neighbor, is a well-maintained seventy-year-old. He traveled half the world, was a top executive at work.

His three children started their families a long time ago and are scattered across the world. His wife goes to visit them. Dragomir is often alone.

When we moved into the building, they both asked us timidly if we would mind the music as they enjoyed playing the piano. They are not very good at it, but ...

I wanted to kiss them!

We are avid piano lovers, just as the trumpet is undoubtedly a dear instrument to them.

Cile is learning to play the trumpet.

A good-natured, sociable couple.

Dragomir is a little more sociable of the two.

He was here and there, saw this and that, is not boastful, does not show off, through his stories he revives and relives events, he is young and strong again, but there isn't enough time.

He appears even younger and stronger when he ends the story with a sex joke.

I'm allergic to such jokes, but his were not tasteless (or funny). They just touch on the topic, indirectly, probing, probably like Dragomir. And they're all the more naive because he generously shares them not only with women, but also with married couples. The children, he insists, have to cover their ears and shout "la-la-la-la-la."

Momcilo, Cile and I are exiting the elevator, and as we were just about to close the door, I hear the key turning in Dragomir's apartment. I'm holding the elevator:

"Neighbor, elevator, will you...?"

"Well, I don't know," Dragomir says mischievously, "How can I interpret this? As a provocation or whatnot? Momcilo, did you hear what your lady said?"

With both feet in the elevator, his head sticking out, we know what follows:

"I have to tell a joke, it's not really ... um, Cile, shut your ears, I'll be quick."

Cile, accustomed to the procedure, like all children from the building, obediently does what he is told.

Dragomir is already chuckling:

"A young woman asks the older man if he will and he tells her—maybe I will, maybe I won't, but I'm willing to try."

Rambo is continuing with his shenanigans!

The poems were not interesting enough for him.

Neither was a birch branch that I dragged into the apartment.

He nibbled on picture frames, TV table corners, shoe cabinet doors, cork photos, cork. He also poked through the box containing paid bills and notices, spilled a can of coffee, and ripped the stuffing out of Cile's toy gorilla.

My aunt is about to have a heart attack:

"Oh, my, oh, my, oh my. What kind of animal is that, it's your fault, you bought it, I've never seen something like this. You will hang a greasy blanket instead of the door, there will be no stone left from your apartment, you will end up on the street!"

I keep quiet and pray to God not to bomb her.

After she leaves, Cile suggests:

"Let's stick a picture of a parrot on the door and write—I GUARD THIS APARTMENT!"

This winter, Sonja, Petar, Momcilo, Cile and I were guests of a remote resort on the Goc Mountain.

There was no one but us and the staff.

We went to have breakfast in our bathrobes and pajamas, with messy hair.

First a shot of honey brandy, then breakfast.

We wandered the hallways, prepared food together with the chef, one evening we held a masquerade ball (hats, sheets, tablecloths), and every night, we put together a play, inspired by the novels of Agatha Christie and Detective Hercule Poirot.

One of us would hide something, and after a detailed investigation, the detective, played by a receptionist with a drawn mustache, would gather the suspects in a long hall, make them sit on chairs and masterfully exposed the perpetrator!

We turned our heads in contempt when offered newspapers.

The only TV set in the dining room did not have sound, and the picture was blurry. Ideal!

We were shining with happiness. Jack Nicholson had nothing to look for in this hotel.

"How is it possible that the occupancy is so low?" Surprised and overjoyed by such a situation, we asked the sleepy, lanky manager of the resort.

Squinting at us with a toothpick hanging from his mouth, he had an answer for us. His own:

"Ah ... Who the fuck knows?!"

We soon learned that this was his view of the world. His mantra.

We hoped that the snow, which, unfortunately, was a no-show, would start falling heavily, cover the roads and make it impossible for us to return home.

We were already cut off from the rest of the world.

Momcilo, Cile, and I walked for miles through dense pine and fir forests. We inhaled cold air deeply.

We climbed to the top of the Vranje Rock (3,700 feet), which was challenging us for days on end, shrouded in clouds and fog.

Marked letters and numbers on trees and stones did not alleviate the fear of an unknown, gloomy environment.

Or spoiled the feeling of triumph when we reached the top.

Conquerors! Blushing cheeks and noses, sweaty and breathless, taller than Neil Armstrong, we regretted that we did not have a flag to split the Vranje Rock in half.

We saw wild boars in the distance.

The howls of wolves could be heard at night.

We came across a ridiculously shallow, meaninglessly wide, fast stream, winding over rocks, boldly placing itself between us and the path across.

Momcilo was throwing in piles of logs that were rolling on the water without any particular order, trying to make a bridge, until an old man wearing boots to his waist appeared, looked at us under his eyelashes, stepped into the water, and pulled out the firewood.

That's why they wear rubber boots ...

Because of Momcilo's "long log jump" action, we were drenched.

Petar fell into the Rasina, an icy river, a little deeper than the stream. Cile ate red bush berries so his stomach hurt. Amazing, fiery red color!

We raced to the resort:

"Be there or be square!"

"Better to arrive late than ugly!"

The locals could be counted on the fingers of one hand, all of them seniors.

"It used to be a wealthy raspberry-growing area, but it's not worth growing them here anymore. The children fled to Kragujevac, Kraljevo..," they told us."It's such a pity. Huge pity! There are no workers left here, there's no one to invest, and the few people who stayed here stayed for their soul."

They were wonderful hosts to us in their houses, offered us coffee, brandy, and raspberry sweet. I gorged on sheep milk's cheese.

They all had dogs, real monsters, who were protecting domestic animals from weasels and wolves.

And maybe also from...

There was a sign across an entire wall in of one of the house that read in large, uneven, red letters:

Dangerous
Dogs At Night
They Jump Let Loose
Go for Jugular

If you wish and find time, visit the Goc Mountain, James.
I know you'll like it.

Ana has workers in her apartment.

They are there to install doors on her kitchen cabinets.

They are Ivan's friends and colleagues who made the kitchen together and are finishing it today.

"It's been exactly a year and a half since they started building the kitchen!" Ana announces.

Ana and I are chatting about local topics, Olja and Jovan are fighting over a computer mouse.

Half an hour to an hour goes by.

Ivan whispers:

"Could you perhaps remember to offer people coffee, drinks...? That would be nice of you."

Ana circles her hips, lifts her skirt:

"I can offer them a real bomb, and my friend is here, she's lost weight, looks great..."

Olja burst into the living room crying:

"Jovan took it from me, I didn't do it first..."

"Mom, she's rude, she started first!," Jovan shouts.

Ana went to settle the dispute, Ivan was making coffee.

The two of us secretly make fun of our husbands.

When shit hits the fan, they "selflessly" let us handle it.

We return the expired milk to the store, which they were duped into buying. We argue with the neighbors who complain about noisy children.

"You go, Ana. If I go out there..," Ivan threatens.

At least that was the case until recently.

Last week, Ivan answered the intercom.

Olja slapped the girl she was playing with in front of the building, because the girl called her "a stupid cow."

The girl's father wants one of the parents to come down.

Immediately!

Ana is in the bathroom, curling her hair, and that takes time.

They are expecting guests—Ivan's relatives from Ivanjica—whom they have not seen for a long time.

Ivan goes down. He's gone for a long time. A very long time.

He returns with the frightened Olja and the police.

Ana drops her hair dryer, burns her thigh, the dryer falls on the tiles and breaks.

Just like Ivan was. Broken.

The girl's father, a judo master, black belt first degree, had the opportunity to show off in front of his daughter and wife.

He fought with Ivan.

Neighbors called the police, the police filed a report. We find out that the judo master also broke his arcade.

The guests were at the door just as Ivan was wiping the blood with a torn t-shirt.

They handed a bouquet of flowers, coffee, whiskey, and a box of chocolates to Jovan. Ana was pacifying Olja.

We would never know what would have happened if Ana's long hair did not require a lot of care.

But Ivan was a hero, even though he was a called-on volunteer. That's the fact.

I throw Momcilo some bait and he hooks on it:

"Look at our Ivan ... All credit goes to him."

"Everyone would do that, he had to go down, he defended himself!"

"He defended his family, broke that barbarian's arcade!"

"So what? Should I wait for Cile to bust some sleazebag's lip, get into fight with him so I can be a macho too?!"

I sit on his lap.

"Dear, forget about Cile, I will take the responsibility. You know how much that goon from the gym annoys me, so there's no reason to wait."

Andjelka and her husband Brane are selling the apartment.

They have been selling it for a long time, for months even, not because it is bad, but because of the astronomical price they are seeking.

The location is excellent, the layout is logical, the apartment is new, has ultra-modern appliances, bought at a time when they had money.

The time when money was abundant and the other time, the one of crisis, is characterized by a short gap and the constant of the latter—not having.

I detest even writing about it.

Andjelka's husband, an honest man, was a successful business owner, then a returnee business owner, and eventually an indebted business owner. He can easily decorate (read uglify) the town center with the IRS's notices.

Andjelka thinks Brane is incompetent.

Brane doesn't think, he knows that Andjelka is to blame for everything, and for their son's skinned knees when he fell off the roller skates.

I feel sorry for them. They are nice and good people, Momcilo and I went through something similar before I closed my shops.

"You threw money out the window, now tighten your belt. You don't even need a belt, use a rope," Brane attacks Andjelka.

"You would like to have another child and you can't take care of the one you already have! Let's go and live in a cave, feed on grass, and drink rainwater!" Andjelka fires back.

The apartment is being sold at such a high price so they can pay off the debts, buy another one, and start from scratch.

Fate is merciful—a buyer appears, the summoned one, enchanted by the apartment, with cash in his pocket, completely unaware of real estate prices. He came from South Africa, where he spent many years working like crazy, saw the apartment online and that was it!

The exchange is carried out to mutual satisfaction.

Andjelka and Brane are chirping. Like newlyweds. They have settled their debts, are looking around to buy a new apartment and will still have money left.

Andjelka is thinking about buying a new car since they sold the one, and she hasn't bought any decent clothes since...

"A CAR! You are planning to buy a car?!" Brane was all fired up.

"There are more important things, priorities. You are, you are... an irresponsible, unstable person!"

"A car! Of course! You can't go without a car nowadays. Did you even think that having a car is a necessity? You're crazy, like I asked you to buy diamonds..."

They are both right. And that's the worst thing.

Four bodybuilders, a high school girl, and I are in the gym. I have weights in my hands, throwing them left and right. I'm doing well. I work out in the rhythm of music.

Sale bursts in:

"You're dropping the weights, huh? Let me show you, you are not sitting properly, straighten your back, take the weight, do not bend down."

"You're playing with your life, boy. I didn't have my morning coffee yet." I really didn't have it.

Sale puts his hands around my waist, he picks me up, spins around, I'm squealing, the high school girl is squealing too. We're louder than the music. He puts me down on.... Oh, no, not the bike!

"First you play then you catch zzzzz's."

"Screaming is a deadly weapon for them. I'm deaf now, bro!" Even the strongmen care.

Our neighbor Dragomir is standing in front of the bakery:

"Our daughter came to visit us with the twins. They haven't been home just under an hour and they're already babbling what they are going to cook. My wife made some meat, it's been falling apart in the brine for two days. When the daughter saw that, her eyes popped out. She doesn't eat 'poison.' Only macrobiotic food. It's crazy house over there. I went out just to calm down a little bit. And buy a meat pie."

"Please, neighbor, don't get close. I'm on a diet!"

"On a diet? For whom? Boys? But not younger than 25... Ha, ha, ha... Not younger than that."

I avoided the joke. Near miss.

"My friend's son works in a company that went bust. He is not paid at all. But, boy, does he like women, almost as much as me.

He doesn't have any luck with money or women... I told him once, "Listen, kiddo (to this old man), you are going to earn a mountain of money and have your own harem, make a sex tape with one of your female colleagues. It can be soft porn, people like to watch that. They pay for that. When you need to distribute it, think of me. And record it too!"

14

Aaaaaaaahhhhhh....

Sometimes you just have to put up with stuff.

Momcilo's mother Radojka is coming over.

Shortly after Momcilo's father died, she married Daniel. Daniel is Slovak. They moved there immediately after marriage. They live in the town of Previdza.

We visited them once and toured an interesting castle built in 1311 in the Romanesque style.

I made an unsavory joke about Radojka: If she hadn't rushed, we could have toured the castles in France...

Since then, she has been visiting us very rarely.

Radojka likes to keep her distance.

She made quite a distance when her wedding coincided with the beginning of the bombing of the former Yugoslavia, which took her to Slovakia.

I expect her to bring cured sausages, Borovicka (juniper brandy), chocolate, and crocodile tears.

Pushes her powdered cheek into Cile for him to kiss it:

"Kiss your grandmother."

Daniel spends most of his time "wasted," speaks occasionally, listens even less (otherwise he wouldn't be able to withstand the situation), has difficulty moving around, and only changes the position of his belly on the armchair—belly hanging from the back, belly as a tray, crumpled belly with decorative pillows, protruding belly, hiding wall paintings with his belly and decorates the walls with it.

His greatest physical effort, not counting bringing up food and drink to his mouth, is carefully digging up funk from his belly button, which then mysteriously end up on his plate.

They are both shocked by the number of new buildings, the shortage of parking spaces, and the prices of gasoline. Prices.

Radojka and Daniel, through no fault of their own, take me back to those terrible spring months of 1999.

Me:

"What do you think? How is this one going to convince us that we have won?"

Milan:

"Sloba-Slobodan? This is how... We won!"

"And the people, they will swallow it?"

"They won't swallow it, but they'll clap."

The emperor's new suit! It's been tailored again and again, without thread.

Graffiti on a house in Petrovaradin: I SOLD THE HEAVENS BUT I STILL HAVE EARTH!

Newspaper headlines: "We will defend our bridges with our bodies." And a joke follows: "The time has come to defend our bodies with our bridges."

Pushing each other on a river raft which, like a walnut shell, the waves are tossing around in all directions.

"Please, God, I hope there's no power outage, please, God, let there be no power outage," I repeated in panic.

There WAS a power outage.

We haven't had running water for over forty-eight hours now. Even skunks would die of jealousy.

Let alone of the stench.

It's evening. The thin candle is burning out indifferently.

Midnight.

I dial the number of the local power company.

"Good evening, Natasha on the phone. I haven't had running water for two days, and now there is no power."

"Could you repeat, please?" says a young male voice from the other side.

"We've not had water for two ..."

"I'm kidding," his voice interrupts me. "What do you want me to do?"

He's joking? I want his brain.

"Please, please, I am asking you kindly, turn on the power. I'M GOING TO THROW MYSELF OFF THE BUILDING."

"What a pity. What floor are you on, if you don't mind me asking?" the voice is having a lot of fun.

I lived on the third floor at that time.

"On the third."

"Young?"

"I just left my mother's womb." Maybe his way is better.

"Well, then we have to react. You have no water, you say? You called us."

If memory serves me well.

"Which part of the city do you live in?" The voice goes on the offensive.

"The Boulevard, near the farmers market." This takes a long time.

"Missus, the power is coming to you, at your orders, in 10, 9, 8, 7, 6 ..." this one is even crazier than I am, "5, 4, 3, 2, 1, WE HAVE LIFT-OFF!"

Light spilled across the room. Dazzling, comforting, soft. It illuminated every corner, dispelling shadows, ghosts and some fear. It gave hope.

I was warmed by the light of that night and the warm heart of one of the workers of the power company.

I will be forever grateful to him.

Tiger

I'm thinking about you

How can I describe you

Worthy of you

The Way You Are

Your movements

Of an absolute ruler

Nonchalant

Safe

Your astonishing strength

Of a warrior

Gentle colors
Of a lover
Your life
No compromise
Tiger
You are beautiful
Perfect
Like wilderness
To which you belong
Tiger
I would give my last moment
To you
With one jump
One bite
To finish everything off
Without hesitation
In an instant

I didn't tell you about Mica the Truth, Jamie.

I'll fix that right away.

A veteran of Novi Sad's bars, a regular guest of new clubs, an irreplaceable hound dog in tracking fun and hot, freshly baked gossip.

I would be unfair not to point out Mica's active participation in painting colorful city stories.

Mica the Truth fought bare-handed and alone, with an armada of heavily armed criminals, knocked down a bull with just his legs, jumped into shark's jaws, and tamed a mustang with his gaze.

Even he laughed his head off how bold-faced his lies were.

Now an abdominal surgeon, then a promising student, the bald Arsa listened to Mica's adventures and fell for every word, lock, stock, and barrel:

"You jumped into shark's jaws!? You mean, like, right in... How did you manage to get out, for the world's sake?"

For the world's sake, I wonder how Arsa became a surgeon, and for the sake of the world, I fear Arsa the doctor, the abdominal surgeon.

He is weak-willed, naïve. Someone will delude him into thinking that stomach can switch places with something else in an instant, that the liver can pass for the kidney...

"You don't know what to think! Cut, snip, alter!"

Patients are fickle too. "They feel pain on the left side, it's stabbing them on the right side, cooperate, say clearly what is wrong with you, he is not a prophet, he has work to do, they have all the time in the world, waiting around forever, crammed in front of the hospital, whining, drama. Who can endure that?! Arsa is not a slave!" Arsa never got rid of the habit of talking about himself in the third person.

That's a real woman (who watches soccer), Jamie.

I digressed because of the story, sorry.

I started telling you about Mica the Truth, so I should end with him too. Not the letter, don't squirm (far be it).

Mica the Truth himself does not trust people, and he takes even the sincerest confession with a grain of salt.

Even the Pope has to answer to someone.

One day, Mica's throne is on shaky legs.

A total solar eclipse is announced. A rare, magnificent phenomenon. An event not to be missed.

The world is in unprecedented anticipation. The elite booked flights months in advance for places that will provide a complete image of the eclipse. Special glasses for the occasion are being bought en masse.

Poorer people can enjoy the spectacle from their "home bases."

Nature has given everyone a privilege.

Everyone?

Unjust, unprovoked, she prepares a surprise for us.

What is honor for the world is a plague for us.

The eclipse of the sun, what a witch's feast, the drunken play of the celestial forces. Devastating consequences, longer lasting than radiation. If not permanent....

For the obedient, there is a cure. And prevention will help.

Stay in your houses, lock up, check if the house is locked, lower the blinds, turn off the lights and the devices. Sit in silence, count the patterns on the carpet, wait for the apocalypse to roar by. Be brave!

What wise averse, fools boast, or something like that, only a few of us, led by stupidity, equipped with old X-ray films as eye shields, meet in the public square that day.

The silence is deafening. The city is eerily deserted. We and pigeons—bird brains (with the exception of Rambo).

The pigeons are shitting here and there, while we are about to shit in our pants.

In a minute, the end of the world will begin, so to speak.

Tijana's sudden scream seriously startles our cardiovascular system.

She screams, howls, jumps. From laughter.

Mica the Truth, with jacket over his head, runs a marathon of his life.

Fully committed to the task at hand, he looks neither left nor right.

Can he even see something huddled in that burqa?

We recognized him by his clothes. He is the only person in the town and its surroundings to be proud of his red calfskin jacket.

After rigorous control of groping, staring, cross-examination, making sure that we did not become mutants, for the first and last time, to my knowledge, Mica the Truth tells the truth with disgust:

"They fucked us!"

Almost the truth.

"They fucked me!"

The truth.

Mica the Truth has been involved in politics for years. Very successfully. Nobody directs him anymore. He is the one who manages nature.

15

The Nublu bookstore is the Mecca of believers in the written word.

It was named after the New Blue Cafe in New York.

Books for everyone's taste and pocket, from all continents, cover the bookstore from floor to ceiling.

If visitors find a book that interest them, they can read it on the spot, without anybody bothering them.

Cile likes it when we go there because he can climb ladders and make a tunnel out of used books.

Most often, I usually dig deep in the corners for such books, the old ones that are not published any more. The more worn out the better, they have passed through many hands, proving their quality.

How can I forget! Smoking is allowed in Nuble.

A book and a cigarette. And yet Momcilo claims I'm ostentatious.

Vita, a girl who is a store assistant there, is also a writer.

She won the award for the best short story at an international young writers' competition in the Netherlands. She failed to publish anything here. Mystery.

Cile wants to know how books are published.

Really, how *is* a book published?

"There are publishing houses. They are not real houses, they are companies where grown up people work."

"What are they doing?" he asks.

"They decide which books will be printed."

"Is printing free?"

"Nothing is free. Whoever has the money and enough luck for publishers to like their manuscripts, their books will be printed by machines.

The owners of publishing houses make an effort, at least they should, to have good quality paper, a nice cover page, and advertising, for the book to be sold. That's how you make money on both sides."

"Bro, mom.... So, even those people who write garbage but have a lot of money can... get that... printed."

"Bro, son, watch your vocabulary. There is a literary policy in all this, but even I don't understand it. Anyone can publish a book, the question is how many and which people will read it."

"And what if noone reads it?"

"A real writer is satisfied if at least one reader understands their message, at the cost of not earning anything."

Cile's jaw dropped to his little belly:

"Mom, brr.... Everyone who wants to become a writer is crazy, a hundred ..., no, a hundred and one percent!"

Hollyhock blossoms in June and July
Summer meadow flower
Extremely tall, up to two meters
Thick green stems
Large petals of irregular shape
Muted subdued colors
Pink purple cream orange red
Grows on the hillsides along the roads
Surrounded by bellflowers chamomile sage daisies
The large bright yellow pestle is shaggy
Sprinkled with a thick powder
Odorless
Bees wasps bumblebees gadflies flies land on it
Butterflies
I like its name its appearance
I love looking at it
And writing about it

You have probably "ripped" one at some point. No offense, James.
It happens to everybody and it's normal.
I personally prefer a short piercing burst of rabid fart.
Breaking wind is good for the intestines, no matter how uncomfort-

able it is for the environment. I categorically state that there is nothing worse than the long-lasting fart stench.

It's the rudest. The most cowardly.

In the bus, in the office, at the hair salon…

Everyone is trying to behave like nothing has happened, but coughing, sniffing, and rubbing our noses betray us.

There is a proverb that goes: "He got away like an ass blast."

Ass blasts. People that are ass blasts.

My granny used to call them "chicken shits."

If you ever lived in a small town, you had a chance of stepping into chicken shit.

Unobtrusive, camouflaged in the grass. It's hard not to miss it.

It is concreted on the shoes as the owner tries to scratch it off, rub it, while drowning in the indescribably sharp stench.

Both ass blasts and chicken shit have a heart marrow like a chicken's ass, with the same function and character.

They are everywhere. They cannot be fucked over.

I can't separate the steaks, just took them out of the freezer. I have to work fast. Momcilo's colleagues from Belgrade are coming over unannounced. I don't like unannounced guests and frozen meat that needs to be thawed urgently. I take a Grand Canyon knife, dig into the cubed, frozen steaks. The ice crunches, I attack again, a large part breaks off and disappears under the refrigerator, I stab, the steaks are sliding on the smooth surface, I trace their fall with my eyes, they end up on my toes:

"Fuck the guests! Cile, don't accidentally say that in front of dad's friends who are coming over!"

There's always some shit happening with house guests.

Momcilo knows Novi Sad. I know Novi Sad.

Different halves. We walked along parallel paths until our paths collided and became inextricably tangled.

We both know Soldier Svejk.

That's how he introduces himself, what everyone calls him. Nobody knows his name. I don't think he knows it anymore.

He is known to have been a special agent. Recently retired.

According to Soldier Svejk, he took part in all the wars. He was security for high-ranking officials and was sent on top-secret tasks in the underground.

Short, stocky, covered with tattoos, in camouflage pants, wearing staple Ray-Ban glasses.

We touch his bullet wounds, three of them, and a long stab scar. He doesn't have a pinky finger on his hand. "It's good that I didn't lose the middle one," he jokes.

We listen to his exploits, some are repeated, some he confuses with others, all are brimming with blood, smoke, gunfire, fog...He always emerges from them as the undisputed winner.

He smuggles branded goods: sneakers, jeans, watches, glasses, good prices. As he says, they "fell out of the back of the truck."

"If anyone dares to touch you, Naca..." he used to tell me.

He was "on the border" for a long time. One day, he plunged in deep.

He is standing at the corner of Zeleznicka and Maksim Gorki streets, speaking into a wristwatch:

"Target spotted, passing by now..."

"Svejk, what, what, who are you talking to?" I am terrified.

"I'm working, I'm watching their back, keep quiet..." He is signaling with his hands to people that only he sees.

I carefully take off his glasses. His gaze is blank, doll's eyes have more depth.

I kiss him lightly on the cheek. His eyes water for a moment:

"I cracked, gone to hell, Naca."

He's looking at the intersection:

"Wait, get away, here they come."

He lives with his medals and a cat.

It's all in vain
They'll kick you
Whatever you are
They'll hurt you
Ignore you
At best

You can twist
You can get by
But there is
Nothing
You can really do
And you know it
Except to tuck your tail
Squealing
To live a dog's life
As befits
An ordinary dog
Amen

Yesterday I fell in front of the Ciao pizza parlor.

On all fours... with all my weight, and I am not light, at the pedestrian crossing. I cut my knee from the blow, tore my jeans, I got nausea and a headache immediately, the traffic light was green for vehicles, I can't move, I'm a living speed bump.

Some drivers were honking, some people walked around me, an old man in a car was shaking his head in disbelief:

"Girl, what's the matter with you, why don't you move away?"

"Well, I'm lazing around little a bit, lying on the road, waiting to bleed out."

I crawled to the pizza parlor, called Momcilo. "The cell phone number you have reached is not available at the moment." I ordered Coca-Cola and ice cubes for my leg, limped back home, bought new jeans today.

If you could start over, Jamie, would you change anything?

Don't rush with the answer. Be sincere. Would you?

Did differently, thought smarter, skipped or added something? Everyone thinks that, "if only I had the experience I have now..."

"Experience! Wise men do not need it!

Experience! Idiots do not heed it!

I'd trade my lake of experience

For just one drop of common sense."

   —*Ogden Nash*

It's awkward to say, but I think Ogden was right.

Sandra stepped on the parrot.

Her parrot. Yellow, white, and blue. Small. Unfortunate.

She carried a washbowl full of laundry to the terrace, tripped on Isidora's sneakers, and flattened the innocent Peca, her beloved parrot. He was flapping around on the carpet, unaware of what has just happened.

"Killer! I'll report you to the animal protection services! Cretino! Imbecile! Jeeeez, who did I marry?! Cile, don't squat near your aunt, go, play, run away from this house!" Bata is shouting.

"Lick it! You hippo!"

Cile is crying:

"Now Rambo has no more friends."

"I don't have them either, she chased them all away, they are better off."

Sandra is quiet, which is very rare. She's picking up what is left of the poor Peca. She is in total shock.

Nemanja takes one blue feather and puts it in his pocket.

Loaded like a camel, an old lady comes out of a shop.

One of her bags rips open and potatoes and onions start rolling on the sidewalk. I bend down and pick them up. Something hits me, I lose balance and fall to the knees.

Old woman's eyes are filled with anger, her voice trembles with rage:

"Keep your hands to yourself, you trash. Help, help, thief!!!"

She swings another bag, and that one rips apart too, apples fall all over me.

Passersby are laughing. Someone kicks her apples.

It's a rare occasion that Cile is out and Momcilo and I are at home. Together. Alone.

We usually wait for Cile to fall asleep, as if children ever want to go to sleep.

22.30.

Cile has been still for five minutes. He is breathing evenly and seems to have fallen asleep. He convinces us otherwise:

"I'm thirsty..."

I bring him water.

"I'm not thirsty for water, I want juice..."

The juice is followed by peeing and the seventh bedtime story.

Eleven o'clock has passed. Cile squirms. He's hot. "Who invented the night?" he yawns, "and why?"

Eleven o'clock was ages ago.

He fell asleep. Finally.

I drag myself to the bedroom. Momcilo is in the bathroom, pouring cold water all over himself, to wake up.

"Shhhh... Reduce the shower pressure, it's too strong," I say.

"What do you mean strong?"

His eyes are half-mast with fatigue. I cover my mouth as I yawn.

"Don't shout so much..."

"Ay, ay, Captain. Do you have any more orders?" Momcilo asks sharply.

"You are impossible! I can't tell you anything..."

"The tone is important, there is a way to do everything."

He's impossibly impossible!

"And time for everything. Midnight is not the time to lecture. Nor for anything else. Good night," I put on my pajamas and turn to the other side.

There are days when I just let go
There are days that I resist
There are days when I have fun
Days when I marvel
Pass me by
Pass through me
Pass

Something wonderful happened.

I've already written to you about Cile's hour-long chats with his friends. You can never have enough friends.

"Who else can I send a friendship request to?" he asks.

"Stefan, Anja, Teica, Leon...," I answer.

"They are already my friends. I need someone new," he says.

"Cile, we talked about this before, no talking back."

Momcilo, always the softer parent, finds a compromise. Cile can send a friendship request to his friends.

Cile sends request after a request. He's counting. Not enough.

Momcilo had a friend, Ivica from Zagreb. They met in the army, visited each other, vacationed together.

Then the war came. Then the war went. Momcilo neither heard nor saw Ivo.

He'll try to find him on Facebook.

As soon as Ivica started searching for Momcilo, he came to Novi Sad on business and wanted to see him.

They are both happy as little children.

Ivo is alive, healthy, married, has a daughter called Sena—who is now Cile's friend.

Have you noticed white, fluffy flowers flying and spinning in the air? You sure have. Maybe you haven't.

They are not poplar flowers, I have no idea from which tree they fall, but it is interesting that they are called "my happiness."

My happiness is beautiful, as it befits happiness, it spins in an unpredictable trajectory, it is always there somewhere, mostly only kids notice it.

Let it be known, let it be known! It doesn't matter it's about ladies, read it, James, without hesitation, especially if you are interested in a certain one and gift shopping is not your strong suit.

When a girl chops wood with an ax in an indescribable wilderness surrounded by snowdrifts, exposed to gusts of wind and wild animals, alone, enchanting, scantily clad... Beware now, she must not lose sight of the use of hand cream, even when shaping wooden slats—twenty-five minutes later.

It was late, I dozed off, I don't know how the commercial ended.

Nemanja and Jovana came to visit us.

They sit glued together on a wide sofa in the living room. They hold hands.

With one hand. Another hand is holding a pizza. They aren't eating.

Their pupils dilated. Eyes beaming. Cooing.

A smile hovers on their lips.

I can clearly see countless little hearts and stars, twinkling and flickering around them. I can almost feel them. Bliss spills over the room. The subjects are the wondrous lands of love.

Whatever happens, they'll never be the same again.

"Nemanja and Jovana are so beautiful," Cile concludes.

Guardians of fire
Don't give up.

16

The Exit festival has started.

Most people from Novi Sad are proud hosts of thousands of foreigners, British, Dutch, Italians, French, Australians even. The city pulsates with laughter, youth, music, the streets are colorful with unusual costumes, masks, flashy wigs. The city lives.

I take Cile and his friend Pavle on a crusade to Petrovaradin Fortress.

I hold their hands tightly. They were fascinated, their floppy ears red with excitement.

They have countless questions. It's good that I can't hear them above the music. We come to less-popular music stages, I keep them away from the crowds.

They are gawking around, are so important and big, their little faces are shining brighter than grandiose spotlights. They are dancing, imitating the movements of performers on stage. When the crowd roars, they cheer too.

They are covered with badges, stickers, picture books about the importance of recycling, and they also have balloons with the handles they use for sword fighting.

Momcilo got them baseball caps with a paper windmill on top, they are running around, looking at each other's windmills:

"They're turning so fast!"

"This is the best night of my life!"

"Me too."

Badges and picture books now occupy an honorable place on Cile's table.

The next day, with scratchy throats, they're spelling verses over the phone, putting together a song about Exit.

Everyone has a silly, reckless, I-don't-know-what-came-over-me monster. I imagine it being shaggy, but it doesn't have to be.

Most people just don't know that, so they are amazed when the monster runs amok. And those aware of his presence will be surprised, and not ...

Hey, you! Over there! Don't fidget, listen and learn!

You have a monster too, dear James.

Monsters are conscientiously lulled by obligations, work, TV series, food, shopping, gossip, food, gifts, food ...

I-don't-know-what-came-over-me has its own rhythm, its only master.

Exit. Two years earlier.

Tijana and I got tickets. We will definitely go, roam around a little bit, dance to reggae and be home by 1.00 at the latest because we both have to get up early. We left early, and at 22.00, we were at the Fortress, next to the one-of-a-kind clock. The small hand shows the minutes and the big the hours.

A group of Brits are chatting next to us. We spontaneously start a conversation.

They are in Serbia for the first time, Tijana's cousin lives in London, we have never been, Exit is great, Novi Sad is fabulous, let's take pictures...

We hug, Tom takes the camera: "Cheese!"

"Forget about 'cheese', we've been nibbling on cheese and crumbs like mice for years, say something else," I said to sound interesting.

For weeks afterwards, Tijana took the cheese off my sandwich and snatched it from my hands:

"Forget about cheese, Natasha doesn't like cheese anymore."

"This time, next year, we'll be MILLIONAIREEES!" she shouted, mimicking the popular British TV series, *Only Fools and Horses*. Tijana was more interesting.

"Hey, that's our show!"

They did not expect the word "our" to be a broad term. They are thrilled.

A thin, tall young man with coal-black hair, wearing a black hat, inserts himself between us.

He's one from the group:

"Edward, Ed."

When we shook hands, there was electricity. I pulled my hand away, and only then did I look him in the eye.

I must have seen him somewhere before, he looks terribly familiar to me.

Ed is a drummer, he dropped out of college, founded a band, composes songs and writes most of the lyrics.

I-don't-know-what-came-over-me began to recite Browning's verses:

> "Why?" Because all I haply can and do,
> All that I am now, all I hope to be,—
> Whence comes it save from fortune setting free
> Body and soul the purpose to pursue,
> God traced for both? If fetters, not a few,
> Of prejudice, convention, fall from me,
> These shall I bid men—each in his degree
> Also God-guided—bear, and gayly, too?"

"Why did you recite that?" he asked me seriously.

I backed away toward the ramparts.

"I don't understand."

"Those verses, they are my verses!"

> "But little do or can the best of us:
> That little is achieved through Liberty.
> Who, then, dares hold, emancipated thus,
> His fellow shall continue bound? Not I,
> Who live, love, labour freely, nor discuss
> A brother's right to freedom. That is "Why."

Ed and I stayed by the clock.

His parents are divorced, he lived with his mother, until recently, now rents an apartment with two friends, has a younger brother, almost Cile's age. Yes, he works. Money is damned and damn necessary.

I spent the next three days with Ed, more precisely three afternoons and evenings.

Momcilo tolerated our common interests and my guides of the city until 22.00. Then I came home.

"Take him to a children's game room with Cile." He met him too. We went to Mickey D's, then for ice cream, he showed him magic tricks.

We gossiped about Hemingway, worshiped Ezra Pound, D.H. Lawrence, Walt Whitman.

Ed was a mature young man. The poet in him did not tear him apart, but only contributed to his peace.

We made love for those three and a half days, consciously and without a specific touch.

A short hug over the shoulder, casual adjustment of the locks of hair, flicking invisible crumbs off the t-shirt, one accidental, painful collision of the heads.

The time has come for Ed to return home.

We stand facing each other.

Everything is somehow murky, my heart is beating fast, my legs are made of lead, my head is in the clouds, I am trembling and being crucified by the words that I don't want to know.

"I didn't want to, I don't won't to hurt you, upset you. I'll regret if I don't ask you... Can I kiss you?"

Ed took off his hat, put his lips on my palm.

I got goose bumps.

We did not exchange emails, gifts, promises. I went home and made pancakes.

I know Ed will find what he's looking for.

The monster's five minutes are up. Six.

We caught each other's scent
Drooled
Panted
Squealed
Growled
Circled
Left

The scents stayed
Spraying the air
That you breathe
That I breathe

It's warm
Melancholy on the green leaves of trees
Latent air charge
Dust trembles on the horizon
Glassy sky
Pensive
Distant more than ever before
Long way to go
And forebodings
Nothing specific
Nothing finished
Short-term weakness
From sudden sorrow
How will it spill out
Bitter fruit
And when

17

Cile went crazy for the book, *The Adventures of Captain Underpants.*

I'm going to the bookstore to get the fourth sequel.

"They're sold out, we ordered more, we expect them to arrive next week, there is one more book left, some pages are missing, if it's really urgent.."

I take out a ten-dinar banknote, tear it up, hand over a half.

It's urgent.

Bata and Sandra had a fierce quarrel.

A long time ago, when Nemanja just learned to walk.

I don't remember the reason, money was the cause.

Bata tore a 100 Deutsche mark banknote into small, confetti-size pieces.

He ran out of the house.

Sandra cried.

I'm dying for Prince!

I'm singing, wearing a torn t-shirt and panties, I'm out of tune, the veins in my neck have popped out, unbridled, cleaning the apartment, the vacuum cleaner tube serves as a microphone, "KISS!" My hair is greasy, hair pins fall out, swirling in front of the mirror, twisting around the vacuum cord, my nose is shiny, greasier than my hair. "KISS!" The phone lights up, someone's calling, I turn up the volume, Rambo is impersonating a hamster in a cage. I can't let him out because of the vacuum cleaner, but would like too.

Alas, Rambo threw himself into the vacuum cleaner. What was

he thinking? Cile's balls are rolling, the vacuum cleaner is humming, I turned on the table disco ball, it spins, throwing colors around, tapping my feet, Cira, the stuffed elephant toy, is laughing, he doesn't even have one eye. Great party, Wednesday, 07/17.

How many times have you made a fool of yourself, James?

Or acted like an idiot, inadvertently?

Hurt others?

Wrongly assessed them?

I KNOW I shouldn't. I do not care. It's none of my business.

I'm boiling inside, the blood pressure is rising, pulsates in my head. Don't Natasha, just pass by, relaxed, remember a verse. Cile's jokes, shut up ...

"LEAVE THAT PUPPY ALONE!!!"

The young man and the girl jump away, both in tatters, the yellow dog, which until recently was whimpering in the corner, weaseled his way out between their legs.

I feel triumphant. I look at them with disgust.

They don't look like sadists to me.

They're more... confused. Frightened, yes, that too.

"Zorica sent us, from Budisava, we've been struggling with the little one for days, he has a skin infection, he's sick..."

I'm a huge ass. An ass! That's me. I'm looking for the Whisperer.

Cile and I are in a taxi, the driver is chatting away. He's sick of his job, drives all kinds of scum, is slaving away for nothing:

"Here, you see, ma'am," he skillfully avoids a cyclist.

"People are... simpletons, rude, God forbid, they are not raised right, have no decency." He suddenly brakes, two women are running across the street. Now he's had enough. He's staring in the rearview mirror. Cile, wearing a baseball cap, is bent over, reading a comic book.

"Is that a boy or a girl?" he asks.

"It's my son," I say.

"Then he won't mind. It's his time."

Taxi driver opens the window:

"Fuck you, you bastards, you suck my cock! You douchebag! Rude!"

Lara is beautiful. Well-groomed, not overdone, has style.

One of the few women who doesn't use her looks to her advantage, and the only one I know without a shred of vanity.

She's a good person, ready to help, homely, bakes pies and strudels, hot, arranged on a tastefully set table.

We shop at the same store, which hums like a beehive when Lara comes out:

"She must have had plastic surgery..."

"You mean surgeries."

"She's always smiling and probably thinks of us as fools."

I see fools.

Last but not least:

"What was her husband thinking!? He's OK, a normal man."

"What did I ever do to those people?" Coffee cups on Lara's tray are shaking because her hands are trembling. "This is not the first time, wherever I appear, some shi.. or ... something ... happens." She sprinkles powdered sugar on the cakes.

She changed three jobs and is unemployed currently. Which suits her husband fine.

He earns great money. "If she really wants to, I'll open a salon for her. She's just feigning, wants to be anxious..."

I'm eating Lara's cakes. They are flawless.

"It's like I'm damned! And I will go to the plastic surgeon, let him disfigure me, maybe then I will live peacefully."

It's not worth it, Lara. You're not from this funny movie, that's all, and you're not damned, you're just very beautiful and uncorrupted. Yes, and financially secure.

Enough for the crucifix.

What movie am I from?

A sunglasses vendor in the street couldn't tell.

Dirty blonde greasy hair, pale, pockmarked face, in a coma, sitting on a folding chair. Headphones in his ears.

"How much are the glasses?" I'm shaking his hand while he slowly regains consciousness.

"These are 500, 700; these up on the top are 900. No, all these are 900, and the ones below are 500. Where are those that cost 700?"

I know that some of those cheap, street glasses can be prescription. I ask him if I could walk around a bit wearing a pair of glasses.

"Listen, they look good on me, but I have the impression that everything is floating around me. Give me another pair."

He looks at me, and whether he sees me is another matter.

"Floating, huh? OK, I'm not in that trip, in that movie," he corrects himself, "but I understand, I get it. Here, try these."

Huge black glasses cover half of my face, blowfly-style.

I'll take them off only when I'm at home.

18

Our phone broke down. I'm calling the post office from Bata's phone to report the malfunction.

A prerecorded, metallic-sounding voice informs me:

"Welcome to the call center. To report a malfunction, press 1." I press it. "To report a malfunction, press 1." I'm punching a button on the phone, my fingernail turns white.

"All operators are currently busy, please wait."

I imagine the currently busy operators. What are they doing?

Talking.

How long does a moment last?

"Hello?" the operator says.

"I'd like to report a malfunction."

"The system has crashed, call later."

The system has fallen apart, it's long gone.

In the afternoon I go through the same procedure.

The system is now functioning.

"When can I expect it to be fixed?" I ask.

"Our teams are in the field, working, according to the schedule that is based on the time and importance of the call, each call. I sent out the information, it's being processed, we'll contact you."

"Now tell me in words that I understand. Only shorter," I say.

"The deadline to fix the problem is five days from the day you report it, excluding weekends." Click.

Before going to bed, I remembered that they will not contact me. My phone is broken.

Novi Sad also has its own street musicians just like the biggest capitals in the world.

They are not as attractive as those from the movies, nor as talented, they will not be discovered by a famous producer from an even more famous music label, there will be no happy end. They don't even expect it. They are playing commercial songs, some are working hard, while no amount of effort will help the others.

One of them, with a big nose, wearing earrings, is a staple on the corner of Zmaj Jovina and Dunavska streets.

Last night I asked him whether he knew how to play a famous song from the movie, *The Godfather.*

James, he's ... I hope that this wasn't his five minutes of fame and that his time is yet to come.

He not only played but also sang that song in a way that neither Coppola, nor Anthony, nor Michael, nor Don from Corleone could have imagined, and if they could have imagined it, their hearts would have stopped because it was beautiful. The audience applauded him, asked for an encore, gleeful, moved, carried away.

I was the one to remember what song that was, I wanted to say out loud.

We traveled through rugged Sicily, picked juicy olives, drank thick red wine, walked the narrow cobbled streets, stretched in the Sicilian sun like cats, melted away by images of distant, beautiful landscapes, in the very center of the city, on the corner of Zmaj Jovina and Dunavska.

I was so sorry you weren't here, James.

Brucia la luna n'cielu
E ju bruciu d'amuri
Focu ca si consuma
Comu lu me cori

L'anima chianci
Addlurata

Non si da paci
Ma cchi mala nuttata

Lu tempu passa
Ma non agghiorna
Non c'e mai suli
Sidda non torna

Bruca la terra mia
E abbrucia lu me cori
Cchi siti d'acqua idda
E ju siti d' amuri

A cu la cantu
La me canzuni

Si no c'e nuddu
Ca sa affacia
A la barcuni

Brucia la luna n'cielu
E ju bruciu d'amuri
Focu ca si consuma
Comu lu me cori

Nino Rota

I'm taking Cile to a birthday party of his friend from the neighbor-hood. He's not exactly Cile's *best* friend, and he has been hesitating all day.

10.15.

"I don't want to go, it's gonna suck."

12.00.

"Did he come to my birthday party?"

15.33.

"I wouldn't miss this birthday party for anything!"

In the elevator, I notice bits of sour cream on Cile's cheeks.

I was so judgmental of moms who licked their finger first and then used it to wipe their children's cheeks. Are they out of water or just out of a brain?

While still in the building, at least no one sees me, I question my views.

I lick my finger, take care of the sour cream, kiss Cile.

He's wiping it away. Wiping it away?

"I gave birth to you, I can kiss you when I want to. My son, bro."

Sandra was offended. She got mad at Bata.

"After twenty years of marriage, shouldn't everything be (in)different?" I ask.

"Come on, don't you start. That runs in your family, a sick sense of humor," she replies.

Bata told her that her tits were like shriveled prunes.

"First, they were like balloons," Sandra scratches the surface, "then, they could only fit into a parachute, now they are..."

She doesn't even want to utter that word.

She's digging further:

"I wore a fur coat last winter. He said I was lucky I didn't live in Bosnia, because they would shoot me down like a bear."

She reached the center of the Earth:

"The first time he came to my mother's place, he was wearing a wreath of garlic around his neck. He didn't find a cross large enough, he told her!"

Bata winks, sneaks up behind her, kisses her neck.

"I find your jokes pitiful, I'm sick of you and them," Sandra pushes him away.

Now he kneels before her:

"Oh, you are the most beautiful among women," he shouts. "I will kiss your feet, drink from your shoes. Pour me that bourbon from the bar, in your boots, I will drink it out of them."

Sandra laughs, sourly, though:

"I'm going to buy a new bra, magic one, they say it shapes the breasts, that it's priceless."

I am not in a good mood today. *Something is amiss.* That is how Nemanja announced his rebellion when he was little.

Amiss, the right word, why, no words, I'm not little, my rebellion will not pass.

I'm calling Sonja:

"I feel like shit today."

"Get out in the storm," Sonja replies.

"I can't, it's not a storm here," I say.

The conversation ends roughly there, I wander around the house, colliding with myself.

Sonja sends a message: "Get out anyway."

In the last attempt to save their marriage, Sonja and her now ex-husband, Marko, found a marriage counselor.

At the first and last session, they were given the following task: "Write down ten things you like about your partner."

"I didn't get to number ten even when before I got married," Sonja commented.

That's a difficult challenge for couples before divorce.

The counselor was fresh at marriage, could not comprehend that ten sometimes was an unattainable number, and was stale in business because he replaced professional literature with people.

Sonja remembered the sentence she had read as she leafed through one of the magazines in the waiting room: GET OUT INTO THE STORM.

I have nothing to lose.

I go outside, the hot air cuts my breath, I walk, it's too hot, I walk, I meet Ivana, she arranged to go on a fast walk Finnish or Norwegian style, with a colleague from work, on the Quay, it's really good, it relieves stress, it's a hit in Europe, she invites me to join in, I'm already walking, I'll just speed up, this is not bad, it's not amiss for me anymore, until the next (a)miss.

Momcilo practices aikido.

The skill of avoiding blows. Using the opponent's power. Developing your own.

One day he comes home from the practice, despondent.

They were practicing, the aim was to do a trust exercise.

It consists in letting the student fall on their back, entrusting the fate of their spine to another student who should catch them.

Everybody failed.

Most of them didn't even try, and those who did—were badly bruised, both "the fallers" and "the catchers."

"Dad, when school starts, come during the recess, let me teach you, we play like that all the time. We throw ourselves hard on our backs, whoever catches us is the winner," says Cile.

We are shocked:

"What happens if no one catches you?"

Now it's Cile's turn.

He is shocked back:

"Nothing, we fall. Then we get up and throw ourselves some more."

I'm on the terrace, it's evening.

A flock of bats flies by.

I am tempted to close all the doors and windows.

I am tempted to open all the doors and windows wide.

Sandra and I are lying on the sofa, it's late, we turned off all the lights, watching *Mad Max* on video.

Alone in the apartment.

Nemanja is also there, but he is not visible, he's growing up and getting ready to see a new world soon.

Max smashed them, one by one, mercilessly.

"Natasha, do you think you saw something?" Sandra asks.

I thought that this movie was an unusual choice for a pregnant woman, they also had horrors in the video store.

"Natasha, Natasha, look!"

Sandra was shaken by the movie. Nothing is happening at the moment, Max is riding a motorbike.

Sandra clings to me.

I can feel Nemanja kicking.

I look harder.

I can't see anything.

Except for the shadows.

One shadow is flying. Without a doubt.

No noise.

It slides through the darkness.

The hair stands up on the back of my neck.

Eternity passes. Or is yet to come.

Max, where are you?

"Wait ... it's ... it's ..." Sandra, with her hippo weight, leans on me, reaches out, turns on the light:

"Bat! It's a bat!"

Ha-ha! The common little shitty bat.

Wild and unpredictable. With claws and teeth.

The bat flew, elegantly, gracefully, performed loops, somersaults, plunged and ascended with ease, unmistakably avoiding obstacles in flight, precious skill, true master, virtuoso, maestro among flyers.

It landed on the curtain.

We could clearly see the fur and the folded wings. It was looking in our direction.

Its eyes were alive, warm, and smart.

It disappeared without us even being aware of it.

What a visitor! What a flyer!

Salute, bat!

My beautiful, dearest darling, old, soft cashmere sweater is ruined, Jamie.

Even Cile doesn't fit in it anymore, it has shrunk so much.

For incomprehensible reasons, I put it in the washing machine, together with the underwear, at the highest temperature.

"Maybe grandmother's garden gnomes can wear it," says Cile the comedian.

Yesterday, Momcilo's dark blue sock dyed that very same underwear.

Today, I tried to bleach out the stains.

The only thing that has disappeared, apart from rational judgment when washing clothes, is my good mood.

Towels, bedding, panties faded like this look depressing. Sadly hanging on the rope.

"What color is this?" I wonder.

"Mouse-fart color!" Cile the ex-comedian says. "Well, that's what Grandma would say."

Grandma would say something else about me as a housewife.

Laughter explodes from me, from god-only-knows which distant parts. Cile doesn't need much to start laughing...

One noble, brave lady lived in Africa and later wrote a book about her experiences. She loved and understood the Black continent.

Her name was Karen Blixen.

I would like to single out one chapter.

Every week, on her farm, she distributed snuff to old black women.

At the crack of dawn, the old women gathered in front of her house, many of them walking for miles and patiently waiting for the gift. They were very quiet.

One Sunday morning, the farm was filled with laughter.

The main servant, in charge of the snuff, forgot to buy it that day.

How it amused the old women! They laughed for hours.

Long after that, when they came across Karen, they would remind her of that Sunday when they walked to her house, with anticipation and desire, there was no snuff. And they would burst out laughing again!

Ana is battling against Jovan's hormones.

He's in middle school, his hairs are growing, voice mutating, he is not a boy or a man.

"I grew up, Mom, you don't understand anything, let me stay out until ten... I can't? Well, I'm not having dinner now! To spite you!"

He snapped at an old woman in front of the building, telling her not to bother him, he's not going to fall from the tree, and the tree will not dry out either.

The old woman complained to Ana.

"She's really a bore. Who is that woman?" I ask.

"She's has no children or a husband, has nobody actually, was married, bled her husband dry, the neighbors say that he moved in carrying suitcases, and moved out with just one bag," says Ana.

"With a bag or in a bag?"

Pensive, she's lights cigarette after cigarette, Ana couldn't care less.

"Get dressed, let's go!" I throw her skirt in her face.

"Where?"

"Somewhere for fun, we all need that."

"Where?" she repeats.

"Somewhere."

Are we vain, James?

We are. I am.

I'm waiting in line at the butcher's.

An unusually long line.

People are fussing, pushing, in turmoil.

One of the few things I remembered in history class.

The term "people in turmoil."

It was repeated in every lesson, in every period, everywhere in the world.

People will always be in turmoil.

The sure-correct answer in a school test.

Perched on my toes, I step out of line, all is as usual—the butcher, the meat.

"Why the hold-up?" I ask.

"They promised a gift to anyone who buys a kilo of meat, and it seems that there is only one left." I can't see who's replying to me.

"Let the next customer get it, otherwise we will stay here until the Judgement Day," I say.

"The butcher won't do that, he'll choose who the gift goes to... He's a crooked man."

People are slandering the butcher, the voices are getting louder, a quarrel is imminent.

"What kind of gift is it?"

I almost got torn to pieces:

"How do I know, child? Stop being such a windbag! Who cares what the gift is?! I am not leaving!"

Should I turn around and leave? I am so close...

"Half a kilo of ground beef, please," I order.

The butcher works quickly, with practiced movements. Gives me the package, looks up:

"Just a moment," he disappears behind the freezer.

He pulls out a red roll, hands it to me with a promising "this doesn't have to be the end" look.

"For you. Because you are beautiful."

I am holding a purse, vanity case, and wallet in my hand. A gift, stupid conceitedness tickles me, makes me smile, I'm singing to myself, looking in the shop window, "Once little and stupid, now big and stupid," I can almost agree with Bata. But I will never tell him that.

Today is your birthday...

Happy b-day, dear Jamie.

Wish you good health, firstly.

Desire, secondly.

Do not rush. Keep it in yourself. Check it. Shape it. Nurture it. Encourage it.

And then set it free. Only one. The true one.

Realize.

19

Every man has his own scent.

Every house.

Every landscape.

Dad smelled of tobacco, cognac or brandy, cologne, Old Spice. He exuded strength and firmness. Persistence. Always present. Never intrusive. When I smell his shirt, I feel calm and protected.

Something in the air smelled of him today.

There's nothing like a scent to revive and trigger memories.

Tomorrow I'm going to Sonja's in Pancevo.

Momcilo needs the car, I'll have to take the bus.

I counted to thirty-one. Sometime after the fifty-fifth try, the bus station phone is no longer busy.

"When does the bus for Pancevo leave tomorrow?"

"15.40."

"Wait, one more question."

"Quickly," the operator probably needs to pee.

"What time does it arrive?"

"Aaaaahhh..." or maybe she's dying.

"Let me see. At 6:05 p.m., according to the timetable."

"That means that it can arrive later than that?"

"Ma'am, how many questions do you have? Yes, that means that. You can never be sure about traffic."

She's alright, she just doesn't feel like working.

"So, we won't have to drag ourselves out in Vilovo," Cile is happy.

Vilovo is a town that we pass through on the way to Pancevo, where we stop for about fifteen minutes to change buses, to Cile's displeasure.

Even when we're driving I can't resist stopping here.

One side of the town is an area of reeds and sedges. Above the stagnant pond, the play of flies and dragonflies is interrupted by children splashing in the water, making water bombs, all wearing white underwear.

On the other side rise endless green waves of hills, sprinkled with colorful, small, field flowers.

When I get out of the car, I step into the velvety soft dust.

I open up. I let peace and snugness envelop me. They enter me, erase my memories, so the only thing left is what I see at that moment.

A dormant, untouched piece.

I hang it somewhere on the side of the big painting I'm moving along on.

If I had super-powers, I would use them to blend in with a color, yellow, all shades of blue, orange. And with a beautiful landscape. To a dandelion, poppy, bulrush for just a moment. And a sunflower.

Not everything has to be said out. Loud.

The true feeling of pleasure is to keep silent
To suppress words in yourself
Roll them over your mouth like candy
And just
Beautiful and important and strong
To feel
To sense
Breathe out
It's hard for me to do that, now, here, they're swarming in my head

I'm thinking of some nice things
I'm thinking of you too
I'm thinking of you
I won't tell you
Shhhh

We get on the bus to Belgrade.

Cile is hungry.

I unwrap a sandwich with ketchup. "Watch out, Cile, WATCH OUT!" The ketchup leaks evenly onto my white pants.

I would scream if it weren't for the screams of the red color of ketchup. The driver takes his place behind the wheel. Alas, wait, I run to the fountain, I shower the pants, the ticket controller hurries me, the driver signals, we need to go, we don't, need white pants, the girl approaches the fountain to drink water, there is no water, the controller shouts, a woman from the kiosk brings soap, rubs it in, it foams, here it is, clean, the controller is pulling me, everyone on the bus hates me, I wet my panties, I smell of blueberries and soap.

"I'm full." Cile ate two and a half bites of his sandwich, one of the passengers snatches the sandwich, carefully wrapping it in a napkin, away from me, then puts it in a bag, shakes it, nothing is dripping out of it, gives back the sandwich.

In Belgrade, we are transferring to Pancevo. The Sahara without oases, it's that hot.

The bus is old, the air is stale, the flies are sticking to the skin, the driver with a towel around his neck, wearing an undershirt, is leaking from the seat.

A barefaced young man sitting next to him is yawning, scratching the back of his head. And has something deep inside his nose.

"Full name," the driver tells the young man. "I give him an ID card, it has all the information, chief, he asks for the address, but I gave you the ID card, I don't care if it has a chip, I don't give a fuck about information, did ya ask for it, did I give it to ya, what d'ya want, no, I can, yes, you can, you are not bringing anybody in..."

Who can, who can't, we couldn't discern anymore...

One of the passengers, urges in a dying breath:

"Hey, chief! If you're gonna go, then go."

In Pancevo, Sonja organized the entire day, i.e. the entire night.

We're going to two parties! Yaaay!

Petar and Cile are sleeping under the watchful eye of Sonja's parents, we are leaving, impatiently, as if we haven't been to a party in years.

Well, we haven't. Children's birthdays do not count.

"Now, you will see my two faces," says Sonja.

"Only two? I have a dozen I know. The rest ambush me," I say.

The first event is Sonja's school friend's birthday party. They do not see each other that often, used to be inseparable, now each has gone their own way, the birthday girl is a debonair woman, a college graduate, has a master's degree, married, with two children, suggests going to a violin concert in "The Garden," a popular performance venue in Pancevo.

The second party is ... a party. No specific reason.

Sonja's friends are from their teenage days, they used to have a really good time, once upon a time. Now when they see each other it's not at all like before...

The party hostess, unadapted, turbulent life, derailings, decays, unmarried, one child living with the grandmother in Germany, has prepared a surprise, swimming in the pool, with or without clothes.

We are going back to Sonja's house.

"I'm glad you have those two 'Is,'" I hug Sonja.

"I never went with any of them all the way in, never, never all the way in," Sonja is dissatisfied.

"Turn around then, let's go all the way in, straight for the pool," I say.

"The pool?" she's unsure.

"The concert?" I am unsure too.

"I would do both," she says.

"No can do. When you are going all the way in..."

"You would like to do what...?" she asks me.

"The swimming pool."

"Agreed," she nods.

"But not without swimsuits," we exclaim in the same voice.

We went home to get swimsuits and fell asleep next to Petar and Cile.

In the morning, sipping on coffee and eating oranges (Sonja's recipe, they go well together, and the colors fit), she confides in me:

"Pedja and I broke up."

"Is it hard for you?"

"No, we knew it would end like this."

"A free woman," I state.

"So, what now? Pancevo is too small for me, Natasha. Narrow-mindedness, envy, drabness..." she says.

"Every city is small in that sense," I say.

Sonja is staring out the window.

"Look, I didn't want you to find out now," I reveal a plan.

Life-saving.

"You and I ... in November ... We're going to Sicily!"

I raise my hand, silence her, I know she's worried about money.

"Momcilo's old friend, a good friend, lives in Palermo. They met at Exit, he invited us to Italy on vacation, to stay with him, whenever we are free. Wait! You will fall in love there, will move there with Petar, I will haunt you..."

"Sicilians are ... short and stubborn ..."

"Okay, then you meet, say, a soulmate, from Japan..."

"In Sicily?"

"Yes, only there. In November."

"A Japanese..." Sonja repeats.

"You are being really difficult, tourists from all over the world go there, so much choice! What wrong with a Japanese?"

"And what's wrong with an extraterrestrial?"

Happiness is where I am not, said the Irish poet, I do not remember the name.

Maybe, really ... Always.

"You open a small boarding house, made of white stone, surrounded by flowers." Sonja cooks phenomenally.

"I wouldn't live in Sicily ..."

"Fall in love in Sicily."

"Does it have to be love?"

"It doesn't have to. It should be."

We are eating oranges, Sonja puts cinnamon into the second coffee.

"Mmmm.... It's delicious.... Seriously, Sonja, we can make Sicily happen."

"I don't mind, on the contrary..."

"So, we took care of you. What about me?" I ask.

"What are you saying?"

What am I saying?

"James! Will he like the letter?"

Sonja stops peeling an orange.

"How can he not like it?! Don't be ludicrous!"

In Novi Sad, as we are entering the apartment, the phone rings.

Sonja:

"And what about when we get back?"

Momcilo's work colleague wants to change his name.

His name is Miroljub.

He thinks that's the problem. It must be.

His wife is a hag, children are impossible, his boss is a terrorist, life is unfair.

"Does he believe that?" I ask Momcilo.

"He doesn't even know himself. He wants to believe it. He can't leave his family, can't find another job, can't finish the house... But he can change his name. Miroljub came up with the idea when he collapsed standing in a long queue. Only people who really wanted to pass him by did so. Before he fainted, he heard the clerk saying, "Why did you let all those people cut the line in front of you? You've been standing here for four and a half hours. Ah, it must be because of the name. Miroljub. Hey, Miroljub!!!!"

Then he fainted.

After a lot of red tape, spent money and nerves, Miroljub (Sissy) became Ratko (Daredevil).

"Ratko is a different man!" Momcilo announces.

"His life has changed radically. He is full of self-confidence, he walks differently, shoulders are straight, his voice is not the same, is rougher, sharper. The wife is calm, sons are little angels..."

"Is that possible?"

Momcilo's laughter erupted in the apartment:

"No, of course it's not. What's the matter with you?! He lashed out at the boss, though he shouldn't have. But it's easier for him now, he claims. Ratko no longer allows anyone to take a parking space in front of his nose. And his posture is different, he's not very hunched over. He is thinking about having plastic surgery, people from the company leaked the story and he took to it."

Pity! I was a little bit hopeful.

20

What's the shortest letter in the world, Jamie?

Victor Hugo wrote it to his publisher:

"?"

The publisher replied:

"!"

Maybe I could have written a letter like that to you, Jamie.

Maybe in our case it is the other way around.

I send you an exclamation mark, you answer with a question mark.

The gym is closed for a whole month.

Sale is going on a vacation with his family.

He found the time. Now, when I have already seen myself as a prominent participant in an international competition, in the men's category.

In the gym, in front of large mirrors, the muscles are tight, the skin cracks under them.

At home...they are...budding timidly.

Momcilo says that his muscles are already well-defined, but I think he is making that up.

Sandra's good friend Ceca, unemployed, her husband, a journalist, part-time as of recently, two girls, two Siberian huskies, won a car.

Under the beer cap, late last night.

It has been confirmed, it's not a fraud, a new car will be delivered to them in five days.

Ceca immediately calls her parents.

Her father answers the phone.

She explains to him, indistinctly, speaks quickly.

Silence on the other side.

"Dad, are you there?" Ceca was afraid that his blood pressure went up at such news.

"Ceca... You're drinking beer at half past midnight!"

I stopped by to see Nemanja, in my role of a stylist. Tonight is an important evening, the occasion is serious, it's not a joke.

Celebration of him dating Jovana. Four months. Full.

Ever since he's been shopping without his mother present, Nemanja's closet is dark.

Shirts, hoodies, jeans, pants, everything is black. Black like coal. Dark black. Black black.

For this occasion, I surprise him with a gray shirt with discreet shades of pink.

He eagerly dresses in the darkness of the room, I can't see him, Nemanja has dark hair and dark complexion, everything is black.

The shirt might have picked things up a little bit, had it not been covered by a black jacket.

The reflection of the gold clasp on his belt reveals his movements.

"How do I look?" he asks.

"Wicked!"

We walk quietly through the living room, Nemanja glances at Bata:

"Hurry up, I don't want to wake Dad up..."

A few more steps and we're in the hall. Bata was a step ahead of us. He fidgets, opens one eye:

"Nemanja ... Nemanja ... You forgot the accordion!"

"I will never fall in love!" Cile is determined. "Girls are prissy and pretending."

"Pretending to be what?"

"That they are... They are... so ..." Cile blinks and twists, "and then they snitch on us to the teacher. First they find it funny then we slide down the railing, then they report us. When Denis and I knocked down the board..."

A little dopey.

"By accident, Mom. Nobody touched it... It just fell."

Tomorrow, he is going to be a big dopey. And with a girl that is pretending.

There is a lovely but cumbersome woman living in the building next to ours—one of those people who always leans toward the interlocu... listener. She is leaning toward Cile.

"Why don't you come over to my place to see my granddaughter, if you only knew how wonderful she is. And you, Natasha, could not stop by for coffee. Yes, you will, nowadays. When is 'nowadays' if I only knew?"

"When pigs fly! Mom said when pigs fly."

There's someone who knows.

The anniversary of Momcilo's and my marriage is coming soon.

Ana suggests that we renew the vows, that we should write them ourselves.

"Momcilo and the written word. What are you on?"

Obsessed with the idea, she takes matters into her own hands.

On the Danube beach, with quiet music and candles in the background, we will validate our love, win over death.

She brought crumpled paper, the color of sand, like parchment.

"I need to fill all this in?" Momcilo turns it in his hands and crumples it even more. "Okay, on one condition! You and Ivan should repeat all that."

"Oh, no, we will memorize our vows," Ana has an even better approach.

Blank paper seems scary to me.

I can imagine how Momcilo feels.

I remember him as a young man.

Slender, like a greyhound, without wrinkles on the outside or the inside, with plenty of thick, strong, coarse hair.

Dynamic, smiling, unique.

"It's nice that you have Dad's hair," I told Cile one time as I was combing it.

Mine is satiny, soft, slippery, as my hairdresser said:

"Pity! You have so much hair and yet it's so thin."

The ex-hairdresser.

Cile protests:

"I don't want to have hair like my dad. He doesn't have hair on top of his head."

I stare in the mirror. I turn. I look closely at my face. I am the same! How does Momcilo see me?

I want to see you the way you are. I want to feel you the way you are. I want to love you because you are you.

I vow to desire, I vow to you, to us, I vow to love, I vow love.

Now and always.

Momcilo played his song on the keyboards, it was intended for me, gave me a shell necklace that he made himself, Ana cried, danced with Ivan who sang, and then Olja, Jovan and Cile began to throw sand everywhere uncontrollably, sand got into Olja's eyes, Ana was scared because the sand damaged her tear duct as a girl, so she had to have surgery, we all drove to the ER together, the doctor rinsed Olja's eyes out, everything was fine, the children fell asleep in the car, we returned home with sand on our clothes and love under our skin.

Have you ever made a phone call while pooping?

Holding the phone with one hand and flushing the toilet with the other? If you haven't, don't. If you have, you won't anymore, Jamie.

Boza, the old slicker.

Married, six children (s-i-x).

Never knew his father, his mother is a singer, drifting here and there, in the Village there is an expression for that, "Wandering around with a mattress attached to her back," Boza grew up in orphanages.

He always fought back, resisted, pushed through, carpenter, painter, barber, graduated collage in his old age, always had a trick up his sleeve, pedal to the metal, fifth gear.

He looks tired today. His face is elongated, shadows creeping over it.

"I have to pay a fine or I'm going to jail for a month. I didn't have a seat belt, first aid was not completed. I don't want to pay, I don't have to pay, I'm going to prison. The judge asks me: 'Do you know what's prison like?' I don't know, but I'm willing to learn. You are not being just, criminals are robbing us in the streets and I am the one going to prison. Because I work like a slave. 'The law,' she says. Maybe. The law of the Wild West."

"So, when are you starting with... additional education?" I ask him.

"Let me tell you, I should have already started it but I didn't show up, no one came to get me."

"Listen, I think your statute of limitations will expire," I say.

"How do you know?"

How could I not know?

A few months after I closed my stores, I rejoiced when the postman brought me a notice from the IRS.

Penalty for failure to issue a cash register receipt when someone bought a newspaper. It had to be paid.

I folded the envelope, I decided to take action.

On the fourth floor of the IRS building, I startle a fat clerk who was napping.

"Oh, hello! Do you want coffee? Please, sit down," he knows me. Everyone here knows me.

"I do not want anything. And I'm not paying this."

"Why, Natasha, it's not that much, you've paying everything regularly so far."

"I won't any longer."

"We will charge you interest on that."

"Charge it."

"Don't mess around, you have to pay..."

"Which part don't you understand? I won't or I won't?"

The fatso looks at me and then the envelope:

"You won't?"

"No."

He opens the drawer, rustles the paper, takes out the donut. Sprinkles it with chocolate crumbs:

"Well, then don't," he says. "The statute of limitations will expire in a year. Wanna bite?"

Boza and I are finishing our conversations, how's the family, the kids, they are taller than him, how tall is Cile?

"He still believes in Santa Claus."

"That's nice. The longer the better."

We have already said goodbye, when Boza turns around, comes back to me:

"I would also like to believe in Santa Claus. If I could believe in anything, I think it would be Santa Claus."

Nemanja explains to me a feature on Sandra's mobile phone:

"And then someone is bothering and smothering you, you press this button, the phone will ring and ring, you apologize, you have to end the call because there's another one on the other line. What do you think?" he asks me, in amazement.

My lucky star.

21

As I'm writing you this, a tiny pale green beetle with transparent wings has landed on the letters.

I would like to assign it some magical meaning, a mysterious message, but I can't.

The beetle is crawling, Cile is reading, Rambo is all listless, he has scabies, it's hot, the clouds are sluggish, they dissipate like withered dandelions, I'm writing, the beetle flies away.

For a long time, my friends and I have been giving each other L.S.A's.

Little Sweet Amulets.

An L.S.A. can be anything and it can have a meaning and carry an obligation.

The plastic figure of Garfield the Cat, Ana's gift, who pours coffee with his eyes half-closed, has demanded from me that I wake up with a smile. I hate mornings.

The silver mirror, my gift to Marina, told her to be beautiful and strong despite the divorce and just because of the divorce.

And it doesn't have to.

Flower, fridge magnet, book, wicker basket.

It is important to be a reminder, make someone happy, smile.

I sent Sonja a t-shirt to Pancevo via a bus driver.

It is unusual and effective.

Sonja's message is the following:

"She is crazy! I'm noticed. I'm going to see *Sex and the City*.

I reply to her:

"You keep forgetting yourself, my dear. You're neglecting your obligation. It has nothing to do with the film *Sex and the City*, think about it, permutate, add, subtract... You'll remember."

A girl from Cile's school was hit by a car.

She suffered multiple fractures, is in the hospital, in a stable condition, has to undergo months of physical therapy.

The driver did not have a license, his girlfriend lent him a car, which she received as a gift from her father.

I have already mentioned that our town is quite small, and we quickly find out that the driver's father is a strict and high-strung man.

"He will beat him dead," the children are chatting among themselves.

Before bed, Cile is restless. He covers himself, then takes off the covers, fluffs up the pillow, crumples the blanket.

"Will he go to prison?" he asks.

"Of course, he will," I reply.

"How so when his dad is going to beat him dead?"

"It's just a saying. Parents don't kill their children."

"I feel so sorry about the girl," Cile says.

"I know, son, we all feel sorry."

"I feel veeery sorry," his lower lip is sticking out, chin trembling.

"Cile, she'll be fine, she already is, the doctors are taking care of her, you'll see her at school in the fall."

"I am afraid she has been punished. When she had a fight with Uroš, she threw his sneaker in the sand," Cile is seriously scared.

"My honey bunny, who would punish her?" I sit next to him, hugging him.

He looks around the room:

"God."

God. Hmmm...

"Do you know what unconditional means?" I ask him.

He doesn't. True, he has some ideas.

"That's how Dad and I love you. Unconditionally, no matter what you do or don't do, absolutely and forever. God has a role, that kind of a role, the only one, he is not a frowning, bearded old man sitting on a cloud, watching carefully what everybody's doing, with a club in his hand. Cile, do you understand?"

Cile tucks his knees under, huddles up, is thinking.

In an instant, he jumps, makes a somersault forward and then one backward.

"I understand now! It's like those funny stories for little babies." He's thinking of the fairy tales we took to the Village.

"Education is what survives when what has been learned has been forgotten."—B.F. Skinner.

When children start school, the period of adjustment begins both for them and for their parents. I don't see where it ends.

Their flaxen hair starts to smell like school.

They get acquainted with the rights and obligations.

They have the right to education.

They have an obligation to obey.

Parents are obliged to pay: money for school activities, insurance, trips to countryside, security. Be sure to read through and give suggestions—should they wear uniforms, and if the answer is "yes," please indicate which parent wants to volunteer to be on call during school breaks. Signature required, also.

The school has rights.

And has rules.

Children should quietly enter classrooms, which were ventilated last time when a broken window glass was replaced.

Before entering, retraining is mandatory. This year, Cile had a thorn stuck in his foot as he was walking towards the board in socks. (He forgot his slippers). Sit still on the chairs. Put the chairs back in place after class. Don't talk to the child next, behind, or in front of you. Don't laugh—it's tantamount to blasphemy—don't push each other in the hallways.

Recess should be spent in silence, noiseless.

They learn poems by heart, and what the poet wanted to say, and the mathematical tasks that the entire family sweats and quarrels over: "Two passengers are moving towards each other at a speed of six kilometers per hour. At the same time, a fly takes off from the nose of the first passenger at a speed of fifteen meters per hour. When it reaches the other passengers, it flies back to the other until they meet. What distance will the fly cover if the initial distance was seventy-two meters?"

They are also learning about the world that surrounds us, the living world in the ponds, the animate and inanimate world in the forests ("Does that mean that ponds do not have an inanimate world?" asks Cile), and the difference between meadows and fields, as well as about the fact that rivers have a right and not only left bank, and also tributaries and distributaries, how to address the teacher, and not resolve disagreements by themselves, how it is not nice to be a tattletale, that they can tell everything to the teacher, that everything is relative, that noise is pain and silence is lovely, that the whole class was writing instead of having a PE class. Here, the whole new world of the latest models of mobile phones was revealed to Cile, with an emphasis on the price.

Cile comes home with a broken nose.

"Why didn't you hit him back?"

"I forgot."

"Why didn't you take cover?"

"I didn't remember that."

"Where was the security?"

The teachers on call are drinking coffee in the teacher room, I know where they are.

Security keeps records. They write down all the inconveniences and then take the records to the school principal. They quarrel with younger children:

"Hey, you! Kid! Yes, you, in green, what did I say, you can't stay in the school yard. I'll write you down!"

They also quarrel with the adults: "We have no authority."

They are equipped with the latest technology. Devices for detecting cold steel and firearms, cell phones.

"Mrs. Natasha, you have a cell phone in your purse," they conclude triumphantly, scanning my purse with some big thing.

Yes, well done, I have a cell phone.

I don't understand why they neglected lighters. At the beginning of the year, the soon-to-be-retired-professor's hair was burned.

A grandfather, who came to pick up his grandson in front of the school, stumbles and destroys the prick, just to fuck with him.

"Do you need help?" the prick offers a hand and grins.

"He doesn't, but you really need it."

He eyes me rudely:

"What can I offer you?"

"Offer yourself a chance."

It's as if I'm sending a child to the battlefield, waiting for his return with fear and impatience, overjoyed when I see him in one piece.

Children are also entitled to penalties (standing next to a bench or in front of the classroom for a more serious offense).

Cile was punished for making children laugh.

Cile and Leon were punished for playing with a tennis ball in the hallway on a short break.

Cile, Leon, and Pavle were punished for pushing a jeep parked in the school yard (a fuckall of a school yard).

Cile and Stefan were punished because they opened the tempera before the art class started, smeared it on the school desk and themselves.

The first thing I see in the Valley, when I turn from the main road to the side road, is a crooked hawthorn tree.

A rusty bird cage is hanging on it. The door was removed. A shaped wooden board protrudes from inside the cage. Birds jump on it, entering the cage to eat berries, seeds, and worms, and come out of their own free will.

Some made a nest in the cage, temporarily usurping it until the eggs hatched and their young were raised.

Their chirping was beautiful! In front of the house we had a real little symphony orchestra.

Milan made that doorless cage.

I'm getting ready to go to the Valley with Cile and Pavle.

Momcilo has back-to-back meetings, so he can't go with us.

But he can go shopping. We are bringing so much stuff with us. Let him carry some stuff too.

I repeat to him several times what he needs to buy. He'll forget half of it.

Momcilo is completely harmless, he forgets everything. Or extremely dangerous, depending on the task entrusted to him.

I also hand him the list, but I know he will lose it.

Every time I go to the Valley, I am overwhelmed by the feeling of Freedom.

The car is filled with the scent of lavender, lilies, mint, wild garlic, lilac, lily of the valley, wild blackberries, raspberries, apples, blue and white plums... a kilometer from the house.

Daddy's roses.

The Valley provides another dimension. Wilderness and expanses. Acacia, the only one in the wider area as far as I know, Milan's pride, has grown, spreading branches full of pale pink flowers, hidden high in the canopy, with unusual fern leaves. It fills the whole landscape with its exoticism.

I can vouch that Milan and his friend Bora discovered the Valley when they disembarked from the boat in what was then a trackless forest.

They cleared two pieces of land, camped, built small houses, and found the place they were looking for—a place to spend their lives, at least his, most of it.

Settlers followed the pioneers.

People of nature, fishermen, buccaneers—too strong a word, let's just say weirdos, different, tired of discipline, a spirit eager for rest and adventure.

Antonija, too wealthy, eccentric in every way, dents her "herd of jeeps," as she calls them, with a cudgel when she has too much to drink, while the Danube carries her hoarse voice:

"It's just a fucking tin, ha, ha, just a tin!"

Ziggy, a misunderstood painter, soaked in paint from head to toe, a would-be-leader of the oppressed.

Stevan, a mad doctor, with a mane of hair, who ran away from his wife.

Ninoslava, sixty-two, topless from April to October: "I came here to blow off steam!"

Grandpa Vasa, grass snakes are his brothers, and brothers feed on milk.

Aksentije, deaf as a post, it's not advisable to go with him night fishing with nets-shotguns. Ten out of ten times he hooks in the river police.

Two or three excellent fishermen who would draw a river if it dried out, and then pull perch and sturgeon out of it.

Houses, log cabins, barracks, villas, sprouting without order, and fences.

And then Gradimir came. And his wife, Vesna. And a lot of giggling, young sisters who, as a rule, fluttered when Vesna was not there.

Every rule has exceptions.

The sky opened, the rain came down, the sisters scampered down the muddy, slippery hill, climbing toward the bus stop.

Vesna was watering her covered garden.

She came to Milan for advice on growing decorative hot peppers. She let Antonija by at the door.

"What a strange woman!" she remarked sarcastically. "They say she doesn't drink only when she's asleep, and she has a hard time falling asleep."

"There's nothing that can be done, my dear neighbor." Milan took a sip of coffee, bringing her a cup as well. "Some drink and some water the flowers in the rain. That's life."

Gradimir loved his sisters and fences. To know clearly what belongs to whom.

He irritated the whole settlement so much so that Aksentije, to whom a tycoon has been offering considerable sums for a house and a plot of land for years, began to seriously consider the idea of selling it.

"On condition that he blocks the passage to that shithead! Well, let him come to his cabin by helicopter, fuck him and fuck everything he is!"

While preparing to set the pegs for the future fence, Gradimir was fenced off.

Dad advised him:

"My old signorina is used to practicing... That fence you are putting up will be a fantastic target. It's just that I'm an old man, my hands are shaking, my eyesight is bad... Think about it, neighbor."

Milan wasn't yet cold in his grave, and the fence was already up.

After the first urge to make a bonfire out of it and ignite it with the fence-builder, I heard my father say:

"Natasha, don't allow yourself to do that. Calm down, wait."

I waited.

Not for long.

On a cold, windy day, I surprised Gradimir.

He was walking around Milan's plot.

"I set up the fence because of thieves, you know."

"What is that? An electric fence?"

"Natasha, I will not stop you from passing through my land."

"How could you? Look where you stand."

His face flared up.

I put my arm around him.

"Gradimir, my neighbor, you haven't been a young man for a long time. You haven't been even happy. This monstrosity is your mirror, Gradimir. You could enjoy the eve of your life in peace, if you could show the strength...to prove... that you have a grain of nobility. Or your downfall will have to be... inevitable."

Gradimir enthusiastically threw himself into cutting and dismantling the fence.

He croaked, purple in the face, slime catching up to the slime, didn't look up, as he was creating his own grain.

He chopped up the wood for the fire. If he measured them with a ruler, he wouldn't match each other so perfectly, by a millimeter, lining them all of them up in Milan's shed.

Every grain sown for the wrong motives is a barren grain.

I just came up with that.

Should I brag?

I'll brag a little bit.

I have been working like a machine.

Mowing. Weeding. Cutting branches. Chopping wood.

This summer, the grass swelled from frequent rain. Mario complimented me:

"You're worth two men."

Mile the Mute, one of Antonija's workers, came over. Such a soft man. Diligent as an ant.

His breath smells of brandy, it's Sunday. He's sizing the mowed grass:

"Well done, Milan's daughter!"

A tide of pride washes over me. And sadness.

"Don't blame me. I miss my namesake. When I used to come around here, I too would put my legs on the table and we would have a shot of a brandy..."

My heart sobbed.

"I'm sorry," he staggered, "I'm not really myself."

"You're tired, just need to get some sleep," I say.

"I'm not tired, I'm pretty drunk."

As I'm weeding my dad's garden and pruning the orchard, I think about how we are all gardeners.

We plant, dig, transplant, pluck, nurture, kidnap, expand the part we got, more, further, we clear the path. For there. Far away. Never close.

Prick your ears, James.

Frogs and crickets sing tirelessly in the grass.

The sun is setting. Herons and bustards are screaming. A piercing, loud scream.

Listen. It's night.

An owlet announces himself briefly, says his name.

Dormice rustle through the walnut branches.

Hedgehogs snort and growl, that's how they call each other. In case you didn't know.

Listen, listen, Jamie.

Dawn is coming soon.

I can hear an ouzel. Woodpecker's blunt blows to the wood. Nightingale sings intoxicatingly. Did you know that nightingales have the ability to imitate sounds from nature?

Do you hear me, James?

The perfect rhythm. Undisturbed harmony. The tom-tom drum of the planet Earth.

The next morning we go to the river island.

Nadja, Mario, Cile, Pavle, and I.

The water is warm, we are lying in the shallows, fish are splashing near us. Nadja makes a cocktail—black beer, Coca-Cola, mint, and ice.

"What's this called?" I ask her.

"Improvisation," she replies.

"I like the way you improvise."

Seagulls are flying above us. Cormorants. They are beautiful.

One bird surpassed them all.

It has a hummingbird's long, narrow beak and the same speed, it's a bit bigger, maybe the size of a swallow.

It flies just above the surface of the water.

I've never seen it quite clearly, it's so fast.

Unspeakably beautiful.

I call it "the blue bird." It's generally called the common kingfisher.

Pavle took out a shell.

"Are there any pearls in it?"

Mario throws it away, over the river sleeve to another river island. They have very sharp tips, like razor blades, he cut himself countless times.

Today, Mario is in charge of lunch.

Wildlife lunch.

He is a magician in finding delicious, fleshy mushrooms like the shaggy ink cap on rotten apples, chicken-of-the-woods, which grow on willows, and the specialties like beefsteak mushroom or crab-of-the-woods, orange-yellow, like a mushroom coral, unforgettable smell and taste, spiced with wild garlic, chives, dandelion, and lemon. Served with fish, of course, whitefish but masterfully fried. I'm already hungry!

"Next time, we will all gather here, you, me, Momcilo, Mario, Ana, James..." I'm counting on Nadja, who's coming.

"James?"

Nadia's not sure how you would fit in, Jamie.

Writing a letter is one thing, but getting to know someone and socializing with them is quite another.

"He's on the same page as us," I assure her.

"I do not know..."

"You didn't read him, that's why you talk like that ..."

Nadja is preparing for a big theater play.

"I can't do it all, I'm losing my mind. Everyone is shitting about the importance of culture, and when it comes to money, culture is transformed into torture. Motherfuckers..."

Interpersonal relationships are also a problem.

Two women, big shots in the city administration, hate each other, and they need both of them and both of them are categorical.

"At least Petrarca saw Laura live," Nadja teases me.

"You don't understand. He can also be an old man, a hermaphrodite, whatever!"

"What do we need a boat for? We'll use your nose to get to the shore," she says.

"Ha, ha, you're a real comedian. And, in the end, to start off with, I imagined it that way. Yes, and for James to be here too," she's really annoying me.

"OK, then. James too," she says in appeasing voice.

Nadja is watching over me. She doesn't want the spell to be broken.

Mario takes pictures of us.

Nadja and I tuck in our bellies, open our mouths.

The camera disappears in the box.

Posing is strictly forbidden.

Mario's good friend, Dimitrije, is a math genius.

In demand across the world, he lectures at the most prestigious universities.

The valley left him breathless.

He drew a blueprint for a house. It will be a shelter when he wants to get away from the windstorms of civilization.

After a bureaucratic whirlwind, already exhausted, and not even halfway through, he was thrown to the seismic ground, having to face bricklayers.

"You have the right to order around, chief, and we have to work. Is there any more cold beer in the crate?"

Calm and always smooth, Dimitrije started swearing. His swear words are light, but swearing is swearing. When Dimitrije says "To hell with it!" it has the same weight as the juiciest, most morbid clusterfuck of fuckery that comes from Jova the Ferryman's mouth.

"He'll get better at it. He's not a learned man for nothing," the construction workers are defending him.

Dimitrije will also learn patience.

"Do they know that I'm paying them?!" he wondered when he realized how long it took to get a phone line.

"Don't worry, just take it easy," he'll learn that too. "You will have to pay here for breathing too. Here you can only get a slap for free."

For a short time, many people claimed he was "theirs" until he underlined that he did not belong to any political party.

The house is finished. Sitting there empty.

Dimitrije chose civilization.

22

"This drop in temperature is refreshing," a shop assistant at the bakery says. "That heat was unbearable!"

A woman who's buying bread disagrees:

"Well, it's summer, when will it be warm if not now, didn't we have enough of umbrellas and jackets?"

They look at each other with contempt.

The shop assistant throws her bread over the counter, a pile of metal coins spills from the woman's wallet, rolling on the floor.

Lazar, my hairdresser's four-year-old son, doesn't understand why his parents are changing their minds about going on a summer vacation to coastline.

He tells them:

"It's not like when we go to the Village to visit and bother them. The sea is calling us to come, I saw it on TV!"

I run into Teodora sporadically.

Married, three children, well-situated.

At school, she stood out with her fiery love songs.

All her relationships were passionate.

She met her husband while studying in Graz, proudly showing off her engagement ring.

Teodora is pregnant, buying baby clothes, kissing her husband.

Love has arrived.

Teodora is pregnant, pushing a pink stroller with a pink baby. Her husband caresses her stomach.

Love blooms.

Teodora and her three children, Irish twins, a golden retriever ties a leash around Teodora's husband's legs, he deliberately falls towards her, kisses her hand.

Love exists. It came to stay.

I'm glad to see them.

They're feeding swans in the Danube Park.

Teodora straightens her husband's tie, he hugs her.

"Children, kiss Daddy! Well, bon voyage, call as soon as you get there," the always smiling, satisfied Teodora.

"Natasha, how are you? You cut your hair short? How are we?! Great! Karlo is going on a trip, the children and I are going to my sister's tomorrow, we will join him later," she waves to her husband, "I can't stand him. You? Everything under control? Cile is still the only child, you selfish mother?!" she pinches my cheek. "Cile, tell your mom... I'll be late, have to go, bye-bye!"

Anxiety digs its claws deep into my neck. It suffocates me for the rest of the day.

Fuck it, Teodora, fuck it!

The phone rings, it's Nadja:

"Tell me something nice, I've been listening to shit all day, tell me you're OK, you don't even have to say anything, just an intermezzo, with someone close, we don't have to say anything."

People often ask the question, "How are you?"

My moods range from elation to melancholy. Sometimes I would like to feel sort of average. Sometimes the thought of it terrifies me.

"Good, not bad," is always my answer.

A notice is stuck on the elevator:

"Don't slam the elevator door, it's not respectful.

The whole building suffers from your arrogance.

Be polite!"

No signature.

The next few days we are all eyeing each other. Suspiciously. There is no one who is not under suspicion. Everyone inquires secretly. Questioning. Lurking. Who is abusing the elevator? Who is the intruder (that we're putting up with)?

Restrained, cold greetings, eyes fixed on the floor. Nobody is comfortable.

The elevator is nurtured like a premature baby. We almost don't use it, and barely touch the door, with awe. We are quieter than ghosts.

A week later, a sheet of paper was put up askew next to the old one: "People, this is bullshit, everyone is slamming the door.

Whoever wrote this notice is a cowardly cunt.

You can find me on the fifth floor."

We breathed a sigh of relief, came to life, liberated ourselves, became polite enough to look each other in the eyes and cordially wish each other a good day.

Momcilo's aunt, Mira, wouldn't hurt a fly. Literally. She apologizes at the grocery store, apologizes when she is paying the bills, apologizes for being alive.

In the apartment, she walks on egg shells, not to bother the neighbors below. Mira weighs next to nothing and can't sleep at night if the children in the yard fought over the ball that day.

She acts indignantly toward Momcilo's mother. Mira saw Radojka's marriage to Daniel as throwing mud at the memory of her brother, Momcilo's father. The betrayal. The grand betrayal.

Mira never mentions her name as if she would invoke evil, dark forces, ready to destroy the planet if she pronounced it.

She heard that Radojka has heart problems, needs a heart bypass surgery and is coming to visit us shortly before the operation, alone, without Daniel. Mira is also close to ending up in the hospital.

"Where she's going in such a difficult time? Even healthy people are biting the dust in the street. Why doesn't she sit in peace? What's wrong with her? Dear god in Heaven, she's only causing problems for herself and others. If she dies in Serbia, it's going to be a big problem for you. Severely ill, but she's going, going, going. Who knows which citizenship she has?! A tin coffin, funeral costs, what a selfish woman, as if you really need all of that and you don't have enough on your plate already."

But Mira is thinking about travelling herself. Ever since she retired, her friend has been selling make-up, pomades, various creams, perfumes. She can't do it anymore. It's too hard for her. And people don't have money. Why wouldn't she treat Mira and herself with a vacation in Vrn-jacka Banja? They have not traveled out of town, let alone out of their neighborhood... It will be fifteen years this winter.

Her friend is hard of hearing. Mira is already swept away by the thought that she will upset the zealous workers on the info-line. I offer to call them.

"Write down everything ... The departure, price, especially the exact price!" Mira is already shaking with travel fever.

But that's nothing compared to scheduling an examination for my aunt with an internal medicine specialist. My aunt does not have a landline in the Village, only a cell phone. Three lifetimes would not be enough for her to pay the bill until she explains to the "brainy" operator that she's living in the Village and yet her medical records are in the city.

The call center, through which, and only so, and in no other way, you can schedule a check-up, is not easy reach on the phone. Before I decide to call them, I equip myself with two packs of cigarettes, and I try to make lunch beforehand.

I remember the day I got them on the first try.

I also remember a kind woman, who spoke meaningfully, listened, without interrupting... She couldn't help me. The doctor was on annual leave, and when he returns, he will no longer work, that is, will only work in a private practice and the clinic has no replacement for him for now. She doesn't know who the aunt should turn to, and if it's any consolation, she is not the only one.

"Please could you tell me on what days are there buses to Vrnjacka Banja, and at what time?" I ask the grumpy person on the info-line.

"And most importantly, could you tell me the price of the return ticket, the exact price, not the approximate one?"

"Why do you need the exact price? That depends on the bus company, it's going to take me the whole day to dictate you all the prices."

"You choose. I don't care about the bus company. I just need the exact price from you."

"Could you please explain it to me?"

"It's not because of me... My husband, you know... It's important to him."

"Why don't you say so? Those husbands, misers, they watch every penny."

Mira thanks me, she's feels sorry that I exerted myself, just ...

"I will not go, Natasha. If someone asks 'where did these old broads get their money from...' She worked on top of her pension. What if they take that pittance from her and she implicates me? No, people will start thinking that we are full of money, get suspicious. God forbid!"

I'm full, I'm brimming with energy, Momcilo is at home all day, let him organize something to do with Cile, I want to be alone, I don't need anyone today, I'm going outside, even a prairie would seem too small to me, I'll wander around the whole of city.

I pass through Svetozar Miletic Street, the statue of Hermes, the Greek god of trade (Mercury, in ancient Rome), on top of Zepter's building, with wings on his helmet and heels, is inevitable. I come out to Zmaj Jovina Street, it's full of people walking by. On Sundays, there are stands with trinkets, young men who exhibit their paintings to girls who are exposing their bodies, couples in love, couples, pensioners, children crawling and climbing on Grandpa Jovan's monument, I'm sure he's pleased, this city of mine is so beautiful!

There is no illusionist who breathes fire and lies on a bed of nails; in his place, a heavy-set man is standing on the pedestal, dressed in plush clothes from the 19th century, a white wig, a blue vest, a white lace shirt, short purple pants, silk gloves, shoes with a thick heel. A true nobleman with his head held high, staring into the distance.

Marina told me about him, how a group of young men insulted him for days, they went overboard, really going for it, until the nobleman in silk gloves showed them that he had fists and balls made of steel. He broadened their horizons. I sit on a bench in Miletić Square, lighting a cigarette and putting on my sunglasses. It's better to be safe than sorry.

All the birds are beautiful, but the pigeons in the town center are too fat, they waddle, do they even manage to take off, people stuff them like geese. Why are they doing this to them, don't they feel sorry?

Mom, child, and grandmother, obviously tired, child is shrieking, pulls mom by her skirt, she ignores him, the little one digs his heels in, grandmother has the "Smack him, don't give in to him" attitude, mom sighs, gently strokes his bottom, grandmother protests: "Not so hard, do ya want to traumatize him for the rest of his life, come to your granny, my precious..."

Coffee to go in Petar Drapsin Street, I wasn't planning on it, but never mind and I don't have a plan, I order a light, refreshing, sparkling, something, "magic drink," says the girl, I have a sip, the sun tilts, a golden drink, I buy cigarettes in the corner shop, I'm given a can of Coke as a gift, a company's rule, there are nice rules too; a little further on, a man and a woman, he roars: "Everyone's shit stinks, including hers, do you understand, everyone's shit stinks, clear?!" It's clear as a day to everybody but he needs a lot of explaining. A young man is giving flyers away, "take your veggie food," brings me into a restaurant, it's interesting, sofas, deck chairs, he opened with his friend on Friday, do I want to eat something, I don't have much money, and I'm on a diet, they give me suggestions, put meals together, they're so young, full of plans, later I come across Dubravka, she's yapping, at first I tried, my back would sweat, now I nod my head, a message from Ana:

"Where are you?" she gets me emotional, asking without any reason, she called home, has been thinking of me. Close to my building I run into Vlada, we've known each other from the first grade of elementary school, pure friendship (saw me with unshaven legs and changing period pads), intense, in high school he moved out of the country, came back, got married, was a football player, now he's a coach, his conscience will kill him, he has to take it, where else could he raise cash for soccer jerseys and balls for kids from the team who kick the ball like they have two left legs.

"No buddy, there's no buddy, your buddy sucks dick, aaah...what are we saying, my buddy, you really got your figure in order... Are you still writing about that... of yours... what's his name... that jackass?"

> I can't sleep
> I go out on the terrace
> The moon is full
> Orange
> Unrest howls in front of the door
> My whole body hurts
> And I don't want it to stop

I want to let go
I want to catch
Whatever that might be
Whatever it brings me

Tijana was looking at your photos posted on the net, James.

"He has colorful eyes. You know what that means," she says. Colorful eyes are synonymous with danger.

"Colorful, but warm, a big oversight," I reply.

"Do you have a book of his?" she asks.

"Don't insult me."

"Give it to me?"

"I'll borrow it."

"You fell in love with him!" she says.

"Did I?"

"Yes, you did, you did," she confirms. "Lucky you! I would also like to be in love." (Tijana has the longest marriage of us all, two sons and a father, all of them eager to tell her how their intestines are working—they want to poop, they pooped, their stomach is acting up...)

A pause, I hear her inhale and exhale cigarette smoke.

"And what if you meet him, and he's the way you imagine him, you want to leave it like that, frozen?"

"I won't even breathe."

The conversations turns into jibber-jabber, I won't even eat, at least I'll be skinny, and if I cry I'll pee less, which will contribute to reduced consumption of toilet paper, which will alleviate the shaken household economy, and who knows, maybe some trees will be saved.

As teenagers, we jumbled together liters of water and dishwashing detergent in my room and blew up balloons for days, trying unsuccessfully to create a star-shaped soap bubble with the help of a twisted wire. Milan choked with laughter and kissed us in our "beautiful, smart little heads." To this day, we have not stopped trying.

Maybe I'm not in love, we conclude, but each of us should be, because that's how everything becomes bearable, even if they're just soap bubbles, it's nice to fly in them, despite the inevitable fall.

"Look how beautifully I fall,

Snow can't fall like that,
I fall low, and I suffer high,
When the middle suffers from height,"

We are quoting Enes Kisovic, although the last verses do not refer to us, we are not in the middle, we do not suffer from heights. We just suffer.

Even that's better than those turkeys from her work, fattened with the pigwash of everyday life.

Or Mona Lisa's smiles of women whose lovers take them to Palma de Mallorca:

"You're missing out, you'll be sorry later, sacred women, transplanting palm trees on the balcony."

Why do they cheat on their husbands? Where do they cheat on their husbands? How do they deal with that? How does that feel for them?

Would I cheat on my husband? If I was sure he would never find out? If I was more than sure I would quickly forget?

If I would? How would I? Would I?

23

Cile and I have been preparing ourselves for the Fruska Gora Marathon (held every year in May) since February, when we found out about it. The preparations have been psychological, jabbering about Fruska Gora, climbers, the appearance of the mountaineering club's booklet with OUR names on it.

Fortunately, the weathermen got it wrong this time, too. It rained the night before the marathon, and the morning dawned washed and polished.

Full of zest, we began from the starting point and start/finish—Popovica.

It's too crowded.

We didn't even count on Momcilo coming. He explained to us that the gridlock would clear up later, everyone will choose their own route, he picked one for us—17 kilometers, enough for the start of the great future alpine climbers.

We are walking on the paths potholed from the rain, the forest smells nice, everything is wet and muddy, we have a good time, the children stop, they make mud cakes, their faces are dirty, clothes too, we will recognize them by their voices, the elderly fall like skittles, there are some hotshots from Novi Sad, they're so smug, boys and girls with backpacks, girls screaming when they come across a puddle, they're helping them, and spraying them a little bit, so they scream even louder, serves them right; so many languages: Czech, this sounds like Polish, this one I know—Romanian.

I was pleasantly surprised by that, the marathon is popular.

We quickly reach the first checkpoint KT1, the mountain lodge on

Glavica, drinking water, we ran the booklets with our names and start numbers through some kind of toothed seal as proof of the journey we covered.

The trajectory and mileage are marked on the back of the booklet—we covered 2.7 kilometers! Whoa!

The next place to rest and get another stamp is on KT2—Stol. 4.1 kilometers to KT7 and the TV tower are still ahead of us.

A standstill in front of us, an obstacle in the form of a small muddy lake. Cile found another purpose for his stick—clapping on it as hard as he could.

"Everyone come here, please gather around!"

A muscular older man with mustache, dressed in an athletic t-shirt and cycling shorts, climbs a stump and raises his arms.

"You can't go on! The pond is too deep!"

That is why he is here, Arnold Schwarzenegger with a mustache, the Terminator of Fruska Gora ponds.

"Don't panic, stay calm!"

The mustache guy has a solution. First he sits on the tree stump. He watches the pond, the pond watches him back. The battle of the nerves.

He will cut two or three trees with a karate chop, shape them, spit again, glue them together and make a raft. No sweat!

We will cross to the other side by midnight the day after tomorrow.

I part with a surprisingly small group, towards a steep, high peak.

"Now we are real mountaineers," I wheeze and push Cile forward.

"Hold on tight to that tree ..."

"If only Bear could see us now, huh, Mom?" Cile's eyes sparkled.

"He'd shit in his pants!"

The ascent is becoming harder, Cile is progressing well, the guys are helping him, pulling him up the slope, who will help me, I'm sliding, digging myself in with my hands, plowing Fruska Gora with my nails, my sneaker gets stuck in the mud, I squirm, someone lifts me, with a strong grip carries me to the top, I can clearly see the sky and beautiful expressive eyes, I thank that person, a half-smile on the other side, why am I blushing, I can feel it, turning around, going down the slope.

The beautiful eyes approach me, casually, as if in slow motion, what did I forget, my child is here, the sun illuminates his hair, he's flexible, walks like a cat, a slightly bigger smile in his eyes:

"The sneaker. You forgot your sneaker."

Shit!

I take the sneaker with my hands dirty from the soil.

Shit!

On KT7, everyone is fed up with the big-assed crying woman, her whining has been following us from the beginning:

"I can't anymore, leave me, go without me, I can't ..."

"You're not even aware of how strong you are," I tell her.

"You think?"

"Take a deep breath and absorb these hills."

I later saw her at the finish line, she was one of the first people there.

Another 4.7 kilometers to Kraljeva Stolica, close to the finish line, and we will become official members of the Mountaineering and Skiing Association of Vojvodina.

The booklet with the drawn heart and the 17 km stamp was well deserved.

I forgot about the beautiful eyes.

In the following days, I ran around the city like a mad woman, looking for white patent leather sandals, I got it in my head that they had to be white and patent leather, both of those. Should I make them myself? Novi Sad is so small.

I met the owner of beautiful eyes at my friends' barbecue.

What was HE doing here, that must be a mistake, the Universe's hellish plan, he owns chains of boutiques all over Serbia, loaded with white patent leather shoes, he gave me his business card, whenever I want to...

I made a wish.

He didn't lie. He had white patent leather shoes.

And charm. And charisma. And a sense of humor. And style.

And those eyes.

A cocktail for under a table.

I uttered the phrase "my husband" whenever he was three meters away from me.

I admit it.

I let him court me. I was flattered, knew it was a game, so I understood it to be pure chemistry, no stars, no newly discovered secrets, no dramatic twists.

I sang and was in an extremely good mood, day after day.

"What's the matter with you?" Momcilo asked.

Nothing special. I found myself a male doll that makes me laugh.

Until he turned into a bloodthirsty clown.

He invited me to come with him on a trip to Geneva. So I can entertain him a little too.

Truly, but truly, Jamie, I didn't expect that.

My cell phone rang. I handle the phone like a red-hot iron. Momcilo: "Where are you?"

I don't know, but I know where I will be soon, where I should be. At home.

I told Tijana about that:

"He knew I was married (not like Lorca, Spanish poet), how could he ask me something like that?"

After the third hour of the debate, the answer is in sight.

"That's why he asked you!"

I can't hit the Universe. I can repel an attack. That's something too.

Marina is miserable.

The company she works for has been sold, her workplace is hanging by a thread, the new owners only shake hands with men, they don't shake hands with women but ...

The company manager is a woman with bleached blonde hair. If she yawns any harder, she'll bite her own breast, a knucklehead, actually being a knucklehead is too lofty for her.

"What am I going to say to Daca?" she's talking about her thirteen-year-old daughter. "Burn the books, my sweetheart. Your mom will pay for a boob job when you come of age so you can swing them in front of some old man's nose while you check his bank balance."

"What about that project with Sinisa?" I ask her.

Sinisa is her former colleague who took severance pay and wants to start a business. He invited Marina to join him.

Marina's laughter turns into hysteria:

"I went to him to show me the machines. There is no trace of the machines, chaos on all sides, a pig sty, I sit on a pile of t-shirts, whatever they are, you're too tense, he says, I've been watching you for quite some time. I'm a great masseur, relax, lie down ... I ... am ... screw... him ... Fuck! Do you think I want that!? You must be fucking joking! There are men like him in droves, with their dicks pulled out and their wallets deflated. To fall for that... at this age... Do not mention that FUCK-TARD to me ever again!"

I was well into my twenties when, at an invitation of an older man, I went to his house to translate some verses for him. He told me he was an ardent fan of the beautiful thoughts of famous writers, he writes them down, what a lovely man, the fact that I knew him under a month did not disprove my conclusion.

I wish I could say that he turned out to be a lout, a slimeball... He made his proposal politely, when I refused, there was no need for keeping me further, he put away a half-full coffee mug, I gathered my notebooks and pencils, not my pride, it flew all over the place, otherwise I wouldn't have asked him:

"You won't write down the thoughts? One sentence would delight you..."

Maybe he thought I was making a joke at my own expense, he escorted me to the door, asked me not to slam the entrance gate because the stones would slide. I didn't see any stones, I did feel them in my head, except for some chaff, it was a rocky ground there.

The sentence he refused to write was:

"Life is like a ball. Wherever it may be, it always hangs in balance."—Erich Maria Remarque. (German writer who created a new literary genre).

Remarque put me back together that day. For the first time.

I'm reading bits and pieces of the letter to Ana.

"I like it very much. It's fierce."

"But?"

"It's like you are addressing a woman, a female in some parts ... Will he...take it as I did?"

James. Jamie. Jamima. I'M KIDDING!

Are you going to take it like Ana? Ana the woman? My dear friend of over twenty years? Who can tell everything from the way I lit my cigarette? Who sees every letter and every word of the letter as crystal clear, close and undeniable?

You will. I have no choice.

Momcilo and I are gradually letting Cile go out to play alone, under supervision from the seventh floor.

"Don't talk to strangers!"

"Don't cross the street!"

"Don't touch the syringes!"

"Don't go into a coffee shop to have water!"

"Don't pet stray dogs!"

He didn't even break a sweat, and he's already pressing the intercom button:

"MOM, MOM, MOM!"

My chest is becoming dangerously clenched, I'm ready to teleport.

"Throw me the ball! The other one! The yellow!"

A company from Novi Sad is on strike.

Chairs in front of the entrance, camping beds, a makeshift table, a hardcover notebook with instructions:

"If you have any suggestions, please write them down here."

"What are they doing?" Cile asks.

"They are demanding their rights, because they think they are jeopardized."

"What rights? Here it says, to life, to..." Cile can get ahead of himself.

"They are asking us for suggestions. Mom, I have a suggestion!" I didn't even doubt it.

"Let's hurry, come on," I squeeze his hand.

"Let him go, ma'am. Let the child say." The women smile at him benevolently.

Cile's face lights up:

"My suggestion is for you to move to Congo! There are gorillas there." We read yesterday about the gentle giants from Congo and their rights are endangered.

"And the gorillas are guarded by gamekeepers, their rights are protected. They are very good and they will protect you. And gorillas are good..."

I really like walking with Cile, I think I wrote that to you somewhere, James. And Momcilo could allow himself to fuck up sometimes too.

I went to a job office.

They organized a course with advice on how to get a job and what kind of work to do.

They put us on chairs, a "suckling" enters the hall with folders which almost completely conceal him.

He arranges them on the table, opens them, turns them over, closes, folds and opens them again.

"Good afternoon," the suckling.

"Good afternoon," the unemployed.

"You may be wondering," he coughs and begins.

"Who the hell hired you?" I think to myself.

"How to find a job? I'm here to help you with ideas and...advice."

I'm worried now.

He's preparing for a running start:

"For example, have you ever considered opening a hair salon? Who among you knows how to cut hair?"

No one. We have someone to get in our hair.

"The following investments are needed to open a hair salon," he lifts his finger. "Minimal!"

Now I find it funny.

After a detailed two-hour-long presentation, we learned the following: we can be potters,

we can be the above-mentioned hairdressers,

we can be embroiderers,

we can be truckers,

we can be whatever we want.

The suckling closed all the folders, wiped the sweat from his forehead, went to rest and withdraw his salary.

"Did you learn anything?" Momcilo asked me later.

"That I had parts of my brain that have not been fucked yet."

Mario finally found the man who screwed him for money. He crashed into Mario's car, flew out of the side street, was guilty according to the letter of the law, was not injured, cried, and begged Mario not to call the police, will compensate him on Friday.

Friday, 365 days later.

"There's no money," says Mario. "He doesn't have it. Not a dime, he says!"

"He has nothing?"

"Small children—he repeated that."

"So, what are you going to do now?"

"I talked to an... acquaintance..." Mario covers his face with his hands. "I can't do that."

An acquaintance guaranteed that he would have his money in twenty-four hours.

"How if he says he doesn't have it?"

"Words are fickle," the acquaintance assured Mario.

"It's not worth it, I won't do that, he has small children, how will he feed them if he's in plaster. Fuck him and the compensation, and me too, and ... I'll see with a friend, he sells good used cars."

In Serbia, Jamie, everything always ends up with "fucking" somehow. Every person is deceived in some way.

"I have great news!" Momcilo has great news.

"Sneza and Dragan offered us to stay at their seaside cabin."

"Fartface and Shitalina?"

"Please don't call them that," Momcilo stiffened.

They're his schoolmates, married couple and work colleagues.

Total fakes.

He knows everything about everything, from how anteaters mate, to a new theory about the Big Bang, pretending to be a liberal, in fact he is weak; she, spiritual, O_2 personified, communicates with flowers and animals, just doesn't reveal what they say.

"Now, give me the tragic news, please," I say.

"It will be good for us, a house on the seaside, we will overlap with them for a few days, they're good people, lower the fences..."

"Fartface and Shitalina have fences up, not me!"

"I've already asked you not use those nicknames."

"Why are you arguing?" Cile asks in a weeping voice.

We looked at each other.

Fartface and Shitalina.

We took off and went for ice cream.

I loved standing between mom and dad as a child, they would hold my hands and swing me in the air. Laughter echoed all the way to the clouds and returned to our hearts.

Sandra and I are washing bottles for tomato juice at the fountain in the Village and putting them in a blue plastic trough.

My aunt is by the cooker, red in the face, stirring the tomatoes in a huge pot.

Sandra drops the bottle and breaks it. Stupid woman!

One slips out of my hands, rolls, hits the rocks around the well, breaks. It is very tricky to wash these bottles, they are very slippery.

Sandra drops another one.

What is it with these bottles?

My aunt scrambles down the stairs.

"Don't help me anymore, come on, move, I don't want to see you near the bottles! Make coffee. It's better."

I'm watching the life of a pack of lions on Animal Planet with Cile. Alpha male, strong, powerful, fearless. Protector, leader by merit.

Females hunt prey in a group, planned, synchronized.

Cubs are taught survival skills through action and absorb every movement of their mother and sisters.

They are all strong, with no excess fat, all muscle and tendons and kill to eat.

They help each other to survive.

Everyone has their responsibilities and knows their place.

They arranged their world according to the laws of nature.

As if they had heard the Dalai Lama's message.

"Mom, that's great, the lioness gave birth to a lot of babies at once, so they can play together," says Cile.

That night Cile quickly fell asleep.

Momcilo and I rushed to the bedroom.

I can't relax. In the middle of it, I start thinking out loud:

"It seems to me that Cile doesn't want to be a single child. I'm ovulating. What do you think?"

"Huh?" Momcilo doesn't think at the moment.

I repeat the question.

"Not now, later..." says Momcilo.

"I'm ovulating..."

"If you want a baby, OK, I am all for it, you know that it's up to you to decide."

Man at work.

"Wait a minute! It's not an easy decision to make... It needs a good think-over," I say.

"Your timing is always impeccable. C'mon, let's enjoy ourselves, we'll reach some kind of agreement by the next month."

Take two.

"Wait! Yes or no? Are we going all the way or...?"

"All the way..." Momcilo moans.

Full steam ahead.

"No!" I scramble, accidentally kicking him in the nose.

"I can't, I'm sorry, I don't feel like it now."

Momcilo got a bruise, Cile won't get a playmate, and I added another notch to the long list of dilemmas.

After our first year of marriage, a urologist diagnosed Momcilo with a low sperm count and motile sperm that is moving in the wrong direction.

Jackpot!

It's due to clogged veins in the testicles, which is easily solved by routine surgery. A year after the surgery, everything will return to normal, the little fools will know what to do.

Even the Olympians did not prepare as conscientiously before the competition as the two of us have, after one year expired.

Step one: folliculometry, ultrasound determination of ovulation.

Step two: "It's me. Come home!"

"Natasha, I'm at work ..."

"Right now!" He still has work to do.

I was already lying on the bed, my buttocks propped up with four big pillows when Momcilo came in.

He went straight to the bathroom, peed, washed himself, washed his hands. Twice.

At full blast, long live hard labor!

When the task is completed, as recommended by the gynecologist, the woman needs to lie still for a while.

After a while, I no longer felt my legs, which were raised in an upright position.

"Please, put the socks on my feet, they are... I believe ... somewhere there," I nodded to Momcilo more with my eyes than my head in the direction of my legs.

"You're not getting up yet?"

I don't think that's deserving of an answer.

"Which socks?" Momcilo roams through the drawers.

"ANY SOCKS! MY FEET ARE ABOUT TO BE AMPUTATED!"

I yell and feel a bit of semen slip out of ... down there.

Escaped!

"If this fails, you will be responsible, put any socks on me or wrap my legs in kitchen towels."

Momcilo finds socks—his own, he is putting them on, pulling them.

"Not so hard, you're jerking my entire body."

This man can't be, shouldn't be normal!

"I've never put socks on someone else. How should I pull them up?"

"As if they were made of cobwebs...glass..."

I know that he would put them on my mouth if he could.

"HA, HA, HA, HA, HA!" I bent over with a burst of sudden laughter, got up, kissed the husband, and called my friends who were waiting for the report.

Two weeks later, Cile announced his existence with a blue line on a pregnancy test.

There is nothing greater than such a miracle. Miracle above all miracles. Creating a new life.

For some time, my aunt felt obligated to point out:

"He's the spitting image of Momcilo. No one could suspect otherwise... Like two peas in a pod!" she said in front of people gathered above Cile in his stroller.

24

There's a book counter in Dunavska Street, in front of the National Library. Used books, 100 dinars each, are laid out on cardboard boxes on the sidewalk.

Books on the counter are not expensive either, from 350 to 800 dinars. It's noon, two booksellers, the sun, the flies, Cile, and me.

"Do you have that...what's his name...a long name... Zelda, a woman and her scandalous life..."

No way, I can't remember.

It doesn't matter much, I wouldn't buy it, I just wanted to chit-chat, as my aunt would say.

"*The Great Gatsby*! He wrote *The Great Gatsby*!"

"You shouldn't have given us so much information, it's over now, you've indoctrinated us. All three of us will remember it at the same time," says the senior vendor.

"And we don't have any of his books," the younger one follows up.

A scantily dressed, attractive girl tests the endurance of her high heels by marching on the concrete paver. A very tall stocky man is trotting next to her. They stop at the counter. She's flipping through some books:

"Do you have the book called *My Boyfriend Is a Doofus*?" She's alluding to the existing novel *My Boyfriend Is a Twat*.

The doofus or the twat, or both, is standing still, letting her act out her little play, he's eyes are kind, he's in love on top of it, will be whatever she wants.

"We don't have a book with that title," the senior vendor says bluntly.

"It's hasn't been published yet," the younger one is trying to pull something.

The girl finds it really funny, taps the stocky guy on the bicep, which is certainly a sign that they should move as they continue to walk down along Dunavska Street.

It was winter, Novi Sad was iced in, the Danube Park deserted.

Cile and I stop at the monument to Djura Jaksic, the Serbian poet, painter, writer, dramatist and bohemian. Cile automatically starts babbling. "Ana pours, Ana serves, but her heart aches for Milo."

White porcelain trees.

Slides and seesaws look lie ruins, they have no purpose.

There are no swans or turtles in the pond.

Just one... duck?!

Right in the middle of the frozen lake.

The duck croaked, flapped one wing, crouched down, and slumped on the ice.

We get closer. One of the duck's wings is stuck under the ice. She's trapped!

"Please, can you come, the duck is stuck in the ice, how can we help her?" I ask the three young men.

They run out to us, take out their mobile phones, recording the duck.

"This is really cool, man!"

More people follow the young men, ages from one to one hundred and one. A decent crowd gathers around.

"Please, I'm a veterinarian, a graduate." The veterinarian, the graduate, stands by the edge of the lake, next to the fence.

"That doesn't give you the right to push me!" An older man was offended and pushed.

"I want to examine the duck. Who the hell is pushing you?"

"Grab it first, bro!"

"Who knows where it came from?!" asks an old woman wrapped in a woolen scarf.

"Well, the doctor will tell you..."

"Don't insult my education..." The vet's nose turned blue, both because of cold and anger. He leaves.

"In my time, everybody knew what you need to do to graduate. And now... If you have enough money..." says the old lady with a scarf.

"Everything used to be different, but now ..."

"What now?" The guy with the camera yells. Behind him is a girl with a microphone in her hand.

TV crew, when did they get here?

"Do you want to get in line? To wait for oil and sugar?"

The old lady shuts up. She wraps herself even tighter with the scarf.

A girl with a microphone fixes her hair. The duck is fluttering its wings.

Men in worn-out clothes are holding a battered bowl from which maze falls out:

"Let's lure it in, it must be hungry."

"Get away, I'm filming, get out of the frame!" The cameraman is beside himself. The vet has returned, throwing snowballs at the duck:

"If she gets scared, she might take off. She must be a wild duck, from the Ural mountains somewhere. She won't last, her beak has lost its color..."

"Oh, the poor duck!" The girls are sorry. "If we could warm her up..."

"You can warm us up," the guys are full of ideas.

The girls are acting coyly, giggling.

"I worked with wild animals for years," the vet says.

"In a chicken coop? You didn't even get a whiff of a wild animal. I'm a hunter, get out of here."

"Mom, firefighters!" Cile spotted them first.

Firefighters, with their heads in helmets! They can't get to the lake, there are too many of us.

"Move!"

The crowd moves an inch.

The girl is talking into the microphone, points to the lake behind her, gets carried away.

The cameraman puts the camera down, she missed it.

"It's gone," he tells the girls.

"Who?"

"The duck! The duck flew away, just as I was thinking of doing a good coverage of the fire rescue operation ... Fuck! Get in the van, I'm frozen!"

"A wild duck from the Ural mountains, a feisty, capable species. I knew it!" the veterinarian puts an end to it.

The phone rings.

"Hello?" I say.

"Good afternoon," someone says back. "I was told I could get the bus station's number from you."

My phone number and the bus station's number match in three digits.

Since I often had to find out about the departure times of intercity buses, I know the info-line's number by heart. I dictated it to a girl after her third wrong call to me.

"Oh, thank you, that's very convenient, the bus station's number is constantly busy," she thanked me and passed it on.

Sometimes you just have to let go... Believe me, James.

Just before the battle, the samurai wrote poems.

Warriors & Poets.

Enchanting.

A scream wakes me up. I sit up in the bed, look at the clock, it's close to 4.00. I'm listening. Maybe I was dreaming. Going out on the terrace, silence, can't hear anything.

This is a relatively quiet area, then again, you never know.

I go back to bed, upset, turn on the TV, *Animal Planet*. Dolphin show. Smiling playful dolphins. Fluffing up a pillow. I don't know when I fell asleep.

Nemanja is at the seaside with friends.

On the first day, he sent me a message: arrived, settled in, everything is OK. The days go by.

I'm at Sandra's, we're talking about everything and nothing.

"Have you heard from Nemanja?" I ask, "How is he? When is he coming back?"

"Why should I hear from him? He's not a baby. I don't want to make an imbecile out of him. He'll come back when he runs out of money," she blew me off.

I'm sure Sandra is thinking of her son. I know she would love to call him. What is stopping her? What is she afraid of?

Love should not be an instrument for restraining children, or even worse, for blackmail, but I cannot shake the impression that showing love is generally classified as a weakness.

The one who openly offers it is a softie, the one who accepts it with open arms is a sissy.

Jamie, if you have kids or are working on it, (I'm pretending I don't know), occasionally tell them you love them. Feel free.

It goes without saying that you show it. It doesn't count without it.

Ziva is packing his suitcases to go to Canada. A friend called him, seasonal work, he needs an assistant.

"What are you waiting for?! Scram!" I say.

"We will talk on Saturday, to confirm, why not, if it is doable then OK, if not—nevermind, I won't go bust," he answers.

"You won't, but it would be better if it is doable."

"Wow, you sound just like my wife," Ziva rolled his eyes.

"Go, work, there's nothing to do here. Let her work a little, enough is enough."

"She works, gave birth to three children, but they certainly don't fall off their bikes when they're on her watch."

Ziva's youngest son, a few meters behind, is lying flat on the sidewalk, a small yellow bicycle on top of him, pedals still turning.

Ziva runs to him:

"Why didn't you call for Daddy?" He lifts him up, puts him back in the saddle, adjusts his little baseball cap.

"Where was I?"

"Work, work."

"Yes! How long should I work? I've been working all my life. I worked and did nothing else."

"Excuse me! You got married, had children. Hellooo! You have a responsibility."

"Is that so? Whoever marries and has children should work until they drop dead?! And then get up from the coffin and help the gravediggers with digging their grave!" he was livid.

"Come on, don't be silly! Just go! I'm telling you."

"Do you women have the ability to listen? It's not complicated and it doesn't hurt, I'll go, I'm going, if he confirms on Saturday. I just told you!"

Yes, yes. To hear him out. To listen.

I already lectured about that before.

I realized that Momcilo wasn't listening to me when, during my, I must admit, monologue, though he inserted an occasional "fuck." That must have been the safest thing for him.

I don't do well at listening to him, either.

BUT

I also don't direct my attention to other things.

When blinded by having to deal with Cile, his school, and extra-curricular activities a whole day, I slumped on the couch and wanted to share that part of the chaos—the car key that got locked in the car when Cile, Rambo, and I got out in front of the vet's, Cile wanted to poop, Cile stepped on the paw of the vet's poodle. With Momcilo, the last thing I expected was for him to grab my ass. Sex is not compensation, and it shouldn't be, it will not erase problems, I won't hop around like Smurfette the next day.

Come on, listen to me. I need you to listen to me.

Not you, Jamie, but Momcilo.

You just need to read. Carefully. And with understanding.

When Rambo just came to the house, he was shocked by our very gaze.

At the pet shop, where we bought him, they advised us to starve him and then offer him food from the palm of our hand. They seemed convincing and to speak from their own experience.

In the beginning, Rambo chose the highest parts of the apartment, the chandelier, the paintings, the tall lamp, if he could, the ceiling.

He quickly began to descend on the shelves, the TV, the mirrors. He did not approach us.

One afternoon, as I lay on the couch, suffering from premenstrual cramps, I felt a stream of air above my head. Rambo flew close to me. Several times.

I closed my eyes, not completely, I looked at him through my lashes.

He landed on the back of the armchair. Then on the edge of the couch. He was watching me. I think he knew I was pretending to sleep.

I spread my palms.

I felt his little legs and soft tail feathers.

I opened my eyes, Rambo was standing on my palm. He looked pleased.

Animals know, James.
Space
Time
Touch
They just know
I open my palm to you, James, here it is:

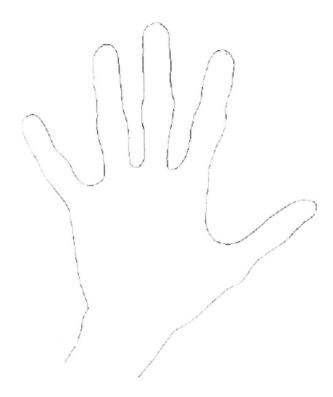

It's a palm. And that's all.

25

My Dad taught me to fish.

Every year he would hang a fishing calendar on the wall with clearly marked months when fishing of certain fish species were allowed or banned. Carp, catfish, pike, bream, sturgeon, silver carp, grass carp... I'm not a fisherman, but I know how to make a fantastic fish chowder.

The secret ingredient goes without saying, Jamie. As well as an invitation to a good lunch.

Dad spent most of his time in the Valley.

Fixing things in and around the house, making brandy, cooking fish chowder, planting flowers, pruning vines, playing cards, continuous, never-ending finishing touches on the boat, fishing, he was not a man of leisure.

He was surrounded mostly by young people, who were attracted to him like a moth to the flame, and just like them, he went to sleep before dawn.

Momcilo and I had the impression that Dad had more friends of our age than the two of us put together.

For his seventieth birthday, I gifted him a book with a dedication: NO ONE CAN DO ANYTHING TO YOU NOW.

"It couldn't be more accurate," he said.

He threw a little party, put on a suit, and bought cherry-colored shoes.

Prepared his specialty, drunken carp.

Ana wanted to make him a cake.

He did not celebrate birthdays before or after that. He celebrated life.

"Well, this is, my beautiful boy, a turning point. From now on, things will happen against my will and management."

"Come on, Dad, don't talk like an old woman."

He looked at me, surprised.

"Not an old woman, Natasha, an old man."

Every summer, he would launch the boat, put Cile on the seat next to him, teach him how to steer, use an oar, tell him about the power of water, whirlpools, waves, big and small fish, predators and prey:

"Never let fear overwhelm you; fear is the worst thing that can happen to a person."

When the doctors told him he had throat cancer, he looked at his watch.

"I'm in a rush to get to the Valley, I have to teach those newbies how to make real brandy. And wash down my throat."

After the operation, the doctor took me aside and explained that the cancer had been removed, but as it was in an advanced stage, there was no other choice but to remove the vocal cords. Milan no longer had a voice. He can learn to speak, but hoarsely, loudly, with effort. Singing was out of the question.

Dad learned to speak, very quickly. Just like the doctor said. He turned down the microphone, dreading anything that wasn't natural. He also lost his sense of smell, so he sprayed himself excessively with perfume and could no longer smoke.

Together, we were shaking the tree and harvesting plums for brandy on a large nylon cover on the grass.

He barbecued more than ever.

He made a house for Cile on a big walnut tree.

He fell down the ladder once. When I ran to help him, he stopped me with his hand, jumped to his feet, shook the leaves off: "My name is Bond, Milan James Bond."

He sang once. Mario couldn't catch the rhythm of the song they were talking about, Milan tapped with his fingers on the table, gave a beat with his foot, put Mario's palm on his heart, and then let out a voice, directly from the heart. The lion's heart.

Everything was supposed to be like before.

He did not launch the boat that summer, didn't even look at it.

I knew. He has decided. He was getting ready to leave.

"Dad, better a live dog than a dead lion."

He patted the seat next to him, inviting me to sit down, and took off his glasses. His gaze was stern:

"If that's how you think, then I made a mistake in raising you. I was not a good teacher. You know better, far better."

We were silent.

"I choose cremation, powder is powder, and this way you won't have a lifetime of upkeep costs."

I got up, made coffee, poured him a shot of brandy.

"Cile is a wonderful child, something will become of him, remember. Be the wind in his sails."

He paused. It tired him out when he talked longer.

He was spinning the glass in his hand.

"Remember that poem?"

I nodded. I couldn't talk, swallow, breathe.

"When the time comes, read it. You can do it. Don't embarrass me in front of people."

I turned my head to the other side. Every atom in me split.

He ran his fingers gently through my hair.

"I had a nice life, Natasha. Life is beautiful. This, now, is torture... One needs to know when the end comes and has to leave with boots on."

"And something else!" He pounded his fist on the table.

I jumped.

"I don't want any bearded men in black! Bring a music band..."

Cile was waiting for Santa all day. And the day before that day. And days and days.

I found a Santa in the phone book. The previous one appeared on one of the TV stations in Novi Sad, and accordingly raised his price.

I didn't know who this Santa Claus was, he seemed fun over the phone, an athlete, worked with children, he wrote down Cile's interests, the names of his friends, "See you on the 29th!"

Milan died on December 29.

I'm staring at the white paper and trying to figure how to put this in words, convey how I felt when they called me.

Santa Claus, Christmas tree, New Year's, snow, wind, stars, there was nothing. Nothingness. Momcilo says I was roaring.

I knew I didn't want to cancel Santa.

And I remember that he sang something to Cile.

The phones rang and rang, friends and relatives came, Nemanja did not move away from me; music, where can I find a music band, I tried, Momcilo called, Bata was looking for it, musicians and acquaintances of a friend's cousin, none, condolences, pre-arranged, impossible, 31st, they feel sorry...

I wandered around the taverns, from the most elite places to the worst shitholes. No one. They were all sold out.

Momcilo called me on the cell phone:

"Santa called, he found the musicians, come back."

In the square, I shouted into the night, I shouted into the Heavens, I shouted into the Why, I shouted for Dad.

Accompanied by the melody "Silently, at night, my precious sleeps," I read the poem:

"O mad, superbly drunk;

If you kick open your doors and
play the fool in public;
If you empty your bag in a night,
and snap your fingers at prudence;

If you walk in curious paths and
play with useless things;
Reck not rhyme or reason;

If unfurling your sails before the
storm you snap the rudder in two,

Then I will follow you, comrade,
and be drunken and go to the dogs.
I have wasted my days and nights
in the company of steady wise neighbours.

Much knowing has turned my hair

grey, and much watching has made
my sight dim.
For years I have gathered and
heaped up scraps and fragments of
things:

Crush them and dance upon them,
and scatter them all to the winds.
For I know 'tis the height of wisdom
to be drunken and go to the dogs.

Let all crooked scruples vanish,
let me hopelessly lose my way.
Let a gust of wild giddiness come
and sweep me away from my anchors.

The world is peopled with worthies,
and workers, useful and clever.
There are men who are easily first,
and men who come decently after.

Let them be happy and prosper,
and let me be foolishly futile.
For I know 'tis the end of all works
to be drunken and go to the dogs.

I swear to surrender this moment
all claims to the ranks of the decent.
I let go my pride of learning and
judgment of right and of wrong.

I'll shatter memory's vessel, scattering
the last drop of tears.
With the foam of the berry-red
wine I will bathe and brighten my laughter.

The badge of the civil and staid
I'll tear into shreds for the nonce.
I'll take the holy vow to be worthless,
to be drunken and go to the dogs."
– *Rabindranath Tagore*

People were coming up, expressing condolences.
"I don't know you," I told the blond young man. "Who are you?"
He leaned toward me and whispered.
"Santa Claus."
Momcilo, Cile and I went to the Petrovaradin bridge. We opened a small urn and sprinkled Dad's ashes. Some of it was carried by the river, some by the wind.
"Stop, Mom!" Cile ordered. "We will not scatter everything. This we'll take home."
In the apartment, Cile wanted to look inside the urn.
"Aren't you afraid?"
"Grandad told me that I should not be scared of fear."
We opened it. Looked inside.
"MOM, DAD, THIS IS THE COSMOS!" Cile exclaimed.
About a week earlier, we were watching a Discovery show about the cosmos.
The bottom of the urn was covered with dark gray powder, sprinkled with red, green, yellow, orange dots.
It was the cosmos.
It was then that I stopped being afraid. I knew I hadn't lost him.
And that no one can lose anyone.
The circle of the dead, the born, the living, those who are yet to be born, includes all of us. We make it. Eternal circle. The circle of the meaning of existence.
James, my friends keep asking when am I going to finish this letter:
"Is there an end to it?"
"Aren't you done yet?"
"She buried herself in it, doesn't even look at us anymore."
"If it's nice, it's enough."
Let this be the end, then, James.

There is one more little thing left.

Your address.

I'm calling the operator:

"I hope you can help me, I'm looking for the address of a writer, only know his full name and the city in which he lives."

"Stay on the line, I'll try to find it, who knows how many are out there," says the operator.

I stay on the line.

"Hello, I have only one registered under that name, write it down. You are very lucky," she added.

Or not.

P.S.

James, Jamie, I think I'm pregnant.

CPSIA information can be obtained
at www.ICGtesting.com
Printed in the USA
LVHW011936300721
693919LV00009B/501